THE

BENEVOLENT

DICTATOR

A NOVELLA BY

TOM TROTT

GW00481970

Part I

I met a traveller from an antique land,
Who said—"Two vast and trunkless legs of stone
Stand in the desert.

Ozymandias, Percy Bysshe Shelley

1

I Meet a Traveller

I USED TO BELIEVE in democracy. I even, for a brief time which I now consider my childhood, believed in politics. Politics is about changing the world for the better, my father would tell me; ever the academic, never the politician. Politics is the art of the possible, is how Bismarck put it. When I say I do not believe in it, I mean it: it does not exist as a force in the world. Democracy and politics are just different ways of describing power; those who have it, and those who do not. Power is very real.

But my story begins before this revelation, when I was still a child. Back then I did want to change the world for the better, and so ever since I was ten I had been unashamed in my quest to be Prime Minister of this island. I would join a progressive party, promote third-way policies, and sweep to victory on a new wave of economic liberalism and social responsibility.

The first step was to find that party. If I wanted to be Prime Minister one day then realistically I only had a choice of two, and being the son of a second-generation Jewish immigrant academic growing up in Croydon, the choice was easy.

So I studied History at GCSE, adding Politics, Philosophy, and Economics at Sixth Form, revising every waking hour to make sure I scored the grades I needed to make it to the best university in the country, and onto the combined PPE degree. I worked hard at University too; bright spring days in the quads were exchanged for long summer nights in the library, and only friendships with the brightest and most tolerant undergraduates survived my habit of blowing off parties to cram. In my precious spare time I volunteered with my local party branch, not that they had a great presence in this university town.

Then, as I approached the end of my studies, a creeping self-doubt infected me that I had nothing special to offer a constituency party, nothing to catapult me up the ranks at the advanced rate required for parliamentary candidate selection. Being a lowly councillor was not my destiny. And so I did what so many before me had done and chose to continue in an academic holding pattern by taking one more year to complete a Masters. And it was as this all too brief year was approaching its end that I learned of "the tradition".

It was a tradition that stretched back almost as long as the degree itself, a public debate between one of us and one of our learned rivals from the *other* university. And it is here that my story begins, as much as this is my story at all. You will appreciate of course why I will try to keep some details obscured.

"Ideology is dead." That was the subject. Our chair of faculty chose the silver ball from the bag, and so I had to argue *for* the subject. I had been selected by him to represent our prestigious university; it was a great honour, he told me. A great opportunity was how I saw it.

A neutral university always hosted, almost always in London, a kind of Boat Race for the mind. It was supposed to be public, that was the tradition, having previously been held in both Parliament Square and Borough Market, but modern times had forced this to be reinterpreted as *open* to the public. In reality, most tickets were sold to family, friends, and the cream of the student union. This was the part that interested me, the union being something of an express-lane to powerful party positions. I hoped I could hitch a lift.

I waited in the wings of the large university hall, a black velvet curtain separating me from the hum and constant coughing of an old and middle class audience. This particular university was what the chair of my course only half-jokingly referred to as a toddler, because it was hardly more than a hundred years old. He and the rest of our side's assembled faculty had left me several minutes earlier to shake hands and share pleasantries with the other old men. It was they who decided which orator had best convinced the audience.

It was convention that the two debaters not be billed by name, but instead by the university whose tribune they were. It had however been leaked to me that my opponent was a man, studying for a doctorate in Middle Eastern History. I rehearsed in my mind the arguments I had concocted to explain why ideology was in fact dead, and tried to imagine what approach a History student would take to argue that it was still alive and kicking. We were supposed to be promoting the art of honest debate, quite what assigning a position on the chosen issue said about honest debate was something I had not yet decided.

It was as I was considering this that Tabby burst through the velvet curtain in the most dramatic way she could manage.

'How are you feeling?' she horse-whispered.

'I'm fine,' I lied.

Tabby was that boyish type of posh girl you still find in abundance when hanging around sixteenth century campuses. If she was a character in an Edwardian novel she would be the only woman in trousers and would be constantly towing a tennis racket. She was the bursar of the college croquet team.

'Not to worry you any further, but you've got some handsome competition,' she said, her voice dripping with glee.

'Are you using handsome in your posh way to mean strong?' I asked.

'No, I mean he's fit as fuck.'

'Great.'

'He's got that swarthy look. Not to mention he's dressed like a sheikh.'

'Fantastic.' That had thrown all my calculations out. 'How do you know what he looks like anyway?'

'I brought him a glass water, pretended I was staff. I was like a proper spy. I could've spiked it, you know.'

I just gave her a look; I was too nervous to engage in witty banter.

She sensed as much. 'You'll be great.' She punched me on the arm. 'And if not, we'll get pissed on the train back.'

'Thanks.'

We heard the muffled *bumpf-bumpf* of a hand patting a microphone: things were about to start.

'T.T.F.N.' she squealed, and zipped through the curtain with another flourish.

Ten minutes later, after a dry speech from the Vice Chancellor of this university, we were introduced, and as I stepped through the velvet curtain and approached the podium, I got my first glimpse of my opponent. He was as Tabby had described: dressed like a sheikh, in white Arab dress, and with a strikingly symmetrical face. We made eye contact as we turned to stand at our podiums, and he gave me a subtle, almost imperceptible wink; his eye did not close, but the muscles quivered. It was classy, and comforted me that he was not out for blood. I tried not to study the sea of faces, my mother was in there somewhere and I needed not to be her little boy. I needed to be Cicero.

Early in the debate I leant hard on my main point: ideology is dead, politics is about what works.

'Look at the health service,' I explained to the audience, 'how many governments in this country have damaged it through slavish dedication to the idea that private providers are either guardian angels or the scourge of the devil? Instead, they should study other systems in other countries, find out what works, empirically, and institute that system.' It was easy to say.

'But there are still fundamental beliefs,' he countered consistently. 'Nations are built on ideology,' he told them.

'How so?'

'Democracy. Despite your convincing argument that politics is about what works, no one in this hall would propose a system outside of democracy, despite its obvious failings. You would not propose a benevolent monarchy because you fundamentally believe that democracy is *right*. Is that not so?'

I thought to myself for a moment. I was here to argue the case that ideology was dead, so avoiding the issue of whether I agreed with it or not, I found myself making the case that convinced some small portion of my soul:

'Maybe you're right,' I sighed, 'maybe you're right. True democracy, with equality of the vote, has only existed in this country for a hundred years, and what has it presided over? A steady decline in this country's influence, and for the first time a generation that will be worse off than their parents. Based on empirical evidence, maybe there is no inherent value in the ideology of democracy.'

Some faces frowned, others laughed knowingly. I was losing the debate. But in my defence, it is much easier to convince people they have principles. I wondered if the union president would recommend me as a PPC on the strength of my argument that democracy does not work. Or my jokes.

After the debate, I walked my mum back to the station, all the time fending off her suspicions that me and Tabby were an item. I could tell her, she assured me.

Once I had convinced her that we were not, I fended off questions of why not. Being an only child I endured the constant attempts to marry me off that would have otherwise been inflicted on a daughter. After that I wandered back to the host university, and where I knew Tabby would be.

The union bar was in a basement of one of the main campus buildings, and had no windows, nor any other sources of natural light, which despite the bright spring days gave the place a constant late-night atmosphere. The entire place, from the furniture, to the bar, to the walls and ceiling, was made of plywood slopped with blackboard paint. Names, numbers, and obscene images had been scribbled on every surface until there was hardly anywhere you could sit or lean without powdering your clothes in chalk.

Tabby was sat on a bench at a table tucked into the nook of the descending stairs. I joined her and the new friends she had made, a fantastic skill of hers, and they all talked excitedly about their plans for life after university. I had taken an extra year to find my answer to this question, but a year is far too short a time to decide the direction of one's life, and although I knew where I wanted to go, I had no idea how I was going to get there. I did not even know what I would do this summer. Returning home to live with my mother in Croydon, finding some dismally underpaid service job, did not appeal. I was set to graduate from university with exceptional knowledge and zero skills.

Our company suggested we continue our fun at one of the infinite metropolitan cocktail bars and clubs available to us, but Tabby could sense my reluctance and kindly declined the offer for both of us. As they ascended up the wooden steps above my head, another pair of more leisurely feet strolled down.

'Oh my god, it's him!' Tabby breathily exclaimed. 'Cooee!' She waved. 'Hello?'

Everyone in the bar seemed to turn, she had an excellent ability to be loud at all times. Standing on the stairs, now wearing jeans and a T-shirt was my opponent. He flashed a winning smile, and stepped down the last planks until he could approach our table.

'Ah, hello,' he said warmly as he spotted me, and extended a hand to shake. I stood up and shook it.

'We have to kiss,' Tabby explained as she offered her cheek.

'I see,' he replied as though it was the most delightful idea in the world, and gave her a quick greeting peck.

'Join us,' she told him.

He did, and studied Tabby for just a few silent moments, a sly grin appearing on his face. 'You're the lady who brought me a glass of water.' He turned to me. 'It was very sneaky of you to send a spy.'

'It was all her, I promise you,' I told him.

'I believe you.' He looked back at Tabby, impressed.

It was like catnip to her. I am not being uncharitable to suggest that Tabby was so confident in part because she felt she had to be. She did not fit our culture's current definition of beauty. There was little feminine about her.

It was because of this, because he had made her feel good about herself, despite very little chance he found her genuinely attractive, that I decided he must be a fundamentally nice man.

'You are a charmer,' she told him. 'Let me get us some drinks, what would you like?'

'Just a beer, thank you,' he told her.

She marched off towards the throng that was now queueing for two-pound pints.

'You did a brilliant job today,' he told me.

'You did a better one.'

'No, I was lucky. I had the easier half of it. If our places had been exchanged you would have beaten me easily.'

Now he was making *me* feel good about myself.

'You're graduating now, are you?' he asked.

'Sort of. In a few weeks, but I've finished my studies.'

'What will you do next?'

'I'm still deciding,' I replied, as though my future hardly mattered, then jumped in before he could probe further: 'What about you, do you finish this year?'

'No, I need one more year,' he sighed, 'but that looks unlikely to happen.'

'Why?'

The smile had gone now. 'My father is very ill, and I will be going back home soon to take a more active role in the family business.' He seemed melancholy, beyond his father's health, as though something indefinite was being taken away from him.

'Isn't there anyone else who can do the job?'

'It's not...' he stopped, thought for a moment. 'My life is on rails. From birth to death my life has already been decided.'

'It's been *planned*. The decision is yours, surely?'

A half-smile seemed to say it was a lovely idea, but a futile one. 'We all have our responsibilities.'

We stared into each other's eyes, with no embarrassing need to look away, entirely comfortable. There was no shame. They were deep, dark brown, with green cracks that showed beneath the surface. Around us the bustle became a muted blur.

'What about you?' he asked, still gazing. 'You didn't answer my question. Your life is free, what are you going to do with it?'

I gave a weak smile. 'I know what I *want* to do with it.'

'And what's that?'

'Politics, of course, I'm a PPE man.'

'Politics meaning... continuing to study it? Journalism? Civil service? Private sector? Prime Minister?'

'Prime Minister.' I made it sound only half-serious.

'Why on earth would you want to do that?'

'Oh, you know, nothing big: just to save the world.'

'SHUT THE FRONT DOOR!'

We both looked round. I knew it was Tabby's voice. She was advancing towards us with three drinks clumsily clutched in her hands. She placed them down on the table inelegantly, slopping a splash of her red wine into his beer, and a splash of his beer into my gin and tonic.

'I've just been told you're a prince. An actual, real-life prince.'

A minute smile of embarrassment crossed his lips, and his face lowered slightly, but did not flush. Tabby plonked herself back down on the bench.

'The family business?' I asked him.

His face came back up crinkled with apology.

'So you're going back home to be king of somewhere?'

'No,' he said definitely, 'my brother will be king, someday. I, thankfully, will not.'

'I can't believe it,' Tabby exclaimed, 'a real-life prince, and here you are in this shithole charming me. Oh! Prince Charming, that's what you are. A real-life Prince Charming!'

Now he was starting to blush. Tabby was still talking at double volume.

'I wasn't trying to lie to you,' he told me, 'I just... it makes people uncomfortable sometimes.'

'What is there to make us uncomfortable?' Tabby asked. 'I'm really comfortable. If they ask us to leave because we're being too loud you can just buy the whole bar. Or the university!—I'm joking, of course. What's your name?'

'Why do I get the feeling I shouldn't tell you?'

'I'm just going to Google you.'

He sighed. 'Amal.'

'Pretty.'

'Thank you, it's a girl's name.'

'Isn't George Clooney's wife called Amal?'

He sighed again. 'Yes.'

'What does it mean?' By this point she was busy typing into her phone.

Another in his range of smiles appeared. This one was a sudden, but cynical, smirk.

'My father gave us all fitting names. My brother's name, Iman, means faith, and my father has always had faith he'll be a good king. My sister's name, Rania, means delighted, and he's always been delighted at how strong she is. And my name, Amal, mean's hope, and he's always hoping I'll do better.'

I read that melancholy in his voice again. Tabby was

too busy reading her phone:

'I've never heard of your country.'

'That's because it's an emirate.'

'What's the difference?'

He shrugged. 'Size.'

'Is that all?'

'We only have around a quarter of a million citizens.'

'So does Iceland, they're still a country.'

'Actually they have a little more. But we only have one city. It is, in reality, just a city, with sea on one side and desert on the other.'

'Don't try and be modest. I'm not princess of jack shit! You are still the richest, and most exciting, person either of us will ever meet. I will be telling people about this until the day I die.'

'I was hoping to be just a doctoral student, enjoying a beer with a couple of other students.'

Tabby thought for a few seconds, before declaring, 'Very well,' as though that was the last word to be said on the subject.

And it was. We spent the next two hours listening to Tabby tell us all about her family, a rather clannish bunch from middle-of-nowhere Kent. He wanted to know every last detail, enraptured by the stories I had found boring the *first* time I had heard them. Their trivial concerns seemed fascinating to him; Aunt Zara's collapsing left wing, Uncle Henry's crusade against badgers, Cousin Xander's "spot of bother" with the law. The time their dog killed Aunt Margaret's spaniel. The time caterers gave a hundred New Year's Eve guests diarrhoea.

I amused myself trying to comically change some of the messages chalked onto the table using a tonic-dipped finger.

Eventually, Tabby announced she was meeting her new friends, and despite desperate persuasion that bordered on begging, Amal refused to join her. She knew I would not be interested, and left, loathe to drag herself away.

'So long, Prince Charming. Send me a postcard from the desert.'

Now alone with him, I moved back to the subject that interested me.

'So how does your country work?'

'How does it work?'

'The monarchy. Constitutional?'

'Absolute.'

I made an interested noise. 'I see, so I was lectured on the value of democracy by a member of a hereditary monarchy.'

'No,' he smiled, 'you were beaten on the subject of democracy by a member of a hereditary monarchy.'

I laughed. 'And just when I thought we had something in common.'

'Maybe we do.'

'Really? So if you were king you would abolish the monarchy and give power back to the people.'

'If it meant I didn't have to be king anymore, in a heartbeat.'

I leant back into the corner, obtaining enough distance to study him in one. He was wearing a t-shirt, jeans, and slip on shoes, just like half the men in the bar. Just like me. But unlike us, every item of clothing was from a designer label. My jeans had cost me twenty pounds, his had probably cost two-hundred. He was trying so hard to be normal, but his nature betrayed him.

'We're a fine pair,' I told him. 'Me, a world away from government, running towards it. You, a heartbeat's distance, running away.'

He smiled, sadly. '"Government is an evil; it is only the thoughtlessness and vices of men that make it a necessary evil. When all men are good and wise, government will of itself decay."'

'Percy Shelley.'

'You're a fan?' he asked.

'Yes. Of his poetry.'

'Then you don't agree?'

'Government *is* the people, you can't separate the two.'

He frowned, unsure. 'For government to exist, someone has to be governed. I think that's what Shelley objected to.'

'People can be governed by good things. Better angels. Shelley was equating government with oppression. One group governing another. Government is everyone working together—*should be* everyone working together. The Roman senate ideal; discussing, agreeing, enacting. Government is not necessary *because* of men's vices; vices and thoughtlessness are the *enemies* of government. When all men are good and wise, then finally government can be unleashed.'

He had not nodded or frowned, or changed facial expression at all during my short lecture, and afterwards he waited for what seemed like minutes until he spoke:

'All this time we've been talking, and I've realised I don't know your name.'

I smiled. 'Ben.'

He nodded. 'Ben, my parents are having a little party this weekend. Would you like to come?'

Would I? I had never been invited by royalty to anything. What was I supposed to wear? What kind of a party was it? How big an affair?

He mistook all these thoughts for reticence. 'You won't have to pay for anything. And we'll pick you up and take you door to door.'

Tabby was right: it would be a story to tell, at the

very least. I said yes. We finished our drinks, and Amal excused himself as he had given his party the slip for long enough and it was best he re-joined them before there was a diplomatic incident. This was all information that meant nothing to me, and that he had failed to mention over the last three hours.

A moment later he had gone, and it was as though he had never been there at all. No one in this university bar had any idea that the lonely young man in the corner by the stairs had this evening become friends with someone who, in just a few months, would be a king.

2

Lifeless Things

I RECEIVED A CALL from the college porter at ten o'clock Saturday morning; there was a man and a car waiting for me. I was lucky, with my hair still wet I just had time to throw on a white shirt, my blue linen jacket, beige chinos, and brown leather shoes: garden party attire, despite the grey day.

As I slipped past the lodge and through the wicket onto the street, the porter watched me with suspicious eyes. I had no idea why, until I saw the long-wheelbase black Mercedes parked on double yellow lines, and the driver waiting to open the back door for me. The porter, whose only experiences of me had involved picking up awkward Amazon parcels and the many times I forgot my key, must have been at a loss to theorise why this bumbling student was being collected in such style.

'Mr Hollow?' the driver asked.

I told him I was, and he invited me to step into the cream-leather backseat. Once snuggled in he asked me if I would like to hear any music, I told him anything classical would be fine. As I settled in for the hour or so drive to London, I pressed a button on the centre console and the seat began to massage me. I had never experienced anything like it.

Numbed, it took me fifteen minutes to realise we were heading north. I was too embarrassed to ask the driver where we were going, but another fifteen minutes later he announced that we had arrived wherever it was.

We trundled through an electric gate, and towards one of two metal hangars. The crisp white pin-sharp nose of a private jet poked out eagerly towards the moody skies. The driver pulled the car up within five metres of the steps, at the base of which stood an attractive brunette in her early thirties, wearing a loose white blouse, sharp burgundy blazer, and matching pencil skirt.

'Good morning, Mr Hollow, my name is Ariadne,' she chirped with a welcoming smile as I stepped from the car onto five metres of laid red carpet. 'If you would like to follow me, please.'

I followed her up the steps and was led into the empty, narrow cabin, and to another cream-leather seat. This one did not offer massages.

'Would you like a drink before take-off?' she asked.

I declined.

'Very well. I'll be your attendant on this flight, so if you need anything, anything at all, make sure to ask.' The way she said it would have aroused a less confused man.

'We're not waiting for anyone else?' I asked.

'The family travelled up yesterday from London. You are our only guest today. Is there anything else you would like to ask?'

'Yes... actually, Ariadne... this may sound stupid, but I have no idea where we're going. I'm not exactly used to this. I've never even flown business class.'

Her customary smile broke into a genuine grin. 'Don't worry, we'll look after you. We're flying to Edinburgh Airport, our flight time will be approximately one hour. Our runway slot is not for another thirty minutes, my advice would be to sit back, relax, and enjoy as much free stuff as you can.'

In less than thirty minutes we were airborne and I could look back onto the Chilterns, and forward to where "England" is painted on the map. I declined a glass of champagne, wanting to keep my head clear, but accepted a Sicilian lemonade. I also accepted a croque monsieur once my stomach started rumbling.

After an infrequently bumpy hour we arrived at Edinburgh Airport in an early afternoon shower. I thanked Ariadne, and was sad to leave her as I climbed into a long-wheelbase black Bentley. It drove me to the other side of the airport, to a spidery midnight-blue helicopter. If I am honest, my heart sank.

Once I had been strapped into my seat, I was given a chunky headset so I could shout conversation with the pilot. Once we were airborne and the croque monsieur had threatened to come back up, I politely asked him how much longer I would have to endure this.

'Flight time today is around ninety minutes,' he told me.

Great.

One hundred windy, stomach-churning minutes later we did a sudden swerve over a large lake and I saw below us several long, connected black marquees constructed right on the bank of the water. They had been erected on a temporary steel floor, anchored into the earth, which gave the impression the tents were floating two metres off the ground. They disappeared behind pine trees as we landed on a similarly constructed steel helipad less than five hundred metres further inland. *Mercedes, jet, Bentley, and helicopter*; I already felt considerably under-dressed.

I was led through the pines by a man in a black bomber jacket until he handed me off to another attractive woman on the land side of the end marquee. This was where the steel floor began, and the woman stood at the base of a red-carpeted ramp that rose the two metres up into the tent.

'Mr Hollow?'

Again, I confirmed that I was.

'Welcome. If you would like to follow the corridor to the end there, it will lead you to the main ballroom.'

I had never heard of a tent with corridors before, but after the ramp the inside was indeed a corridor with canvas walls. On the left were openings that led into rooms, but with periscoped entrance corridors of their own to provide the privacy that a lack of doors normally prevents. As I approached the end of the ten-metre corridor it opened onto the main space of the marquees: two hundred metres of airtight black canvas running parallel to the lakeside; and along that side, polished plastic windows looked out onto the rippling water, and to where the pine-dappled slopes rolled down into mist.

The space was filled with over a hundred people, clusters of men and women, sitting and standing, mostly wearing expensive suits and gowns, some wearing traditional Arab dress. Before I had a chance to scan the crowd for Amal, a waiter appeared at my elbow:

'Champagne, sir?'

I thanked him as I took one of the crystal flutes from the mirrored silver tray, then I began to weave my way through the mass. The guests had an old-fashioned approach to displaying wealth, every one exhibiting some form of gold: earrings, necklace, tie bar, watch; I was not even wearing cufflinks.

As I threaded myself between backs and shoulders I picked up a few snatches of conversation that were not obscured behind thick accents:

'The season has been terrible this year.'

'I just chase the weather.'

'You *must* come to Monte Carlo!'

'It's at least forty feet bigger than the jetty!'

At the other end of the marquee was a staffed bar, all inclusive. One bottle of any of the spirits would cost more to buy than my monthly food budget. I only learned now that the champagne I was drinking was older than me.

I could not see Amal anywhere, so I returned to the windows, by a man seated alone on a brown leather sofa, and stared out over the lake.

The sky was angrier up here in Scotland than it had been in England, and waves were gliding calmly but quickly over the surface of the water. Mist had rolled from the banks, out onto the water, now obscuring the other side of the lake and stretching the view into infinity. I must have been staring at it for ten minutes before the man seated on the sofa commented.

'Desolate, isn't it.'

'Beautiful,' I replied.

'Yes. Harsh but serene. And still Lomond is better.'

I turned to acknowledge him. He looked so relaxed he might have been delivered with the sofa. His legs were crossed in a cream, if not slightly green, silk suit; cream shirt, ascot tie, and a glass of whisky moulded to his hand. His hair was black and his face was as brown and wrinkled as the leather.

'I don't even know where we are,' I told him.

'That's Loch Ness.'

I looked back at it with fresh eyes, but it looked the same.

'And do you know why we're at Loch Ness and not the vastly superior Loch Lomond, my friend?'

'Why?'

'Because these people have no fucking taste,' he growled. 'And when they go to the *next* party they can say they were at *this* party and when they say it was on the banks of Loch Ness other ignorant people will know where that is. They will say "ooh, how quaint" and ask if they saw the monster. Idiots. These people don't go anywhere to *be* there, they go to say they've been.' He paused, giving a measured look to my clothes. 'But not you. Who are you?'

'I'm nobody.'

'Really? Impressive.'

I smirked. 'Is it?'

'Everyone else is here because they're *somebody*. To be nobody and get an invite is very impressive. Nobody who's nobody gets to drink Dom Pérignon 1990 on their dime, you must really be somebody.'

'I see. Are you somebody?'

'I am. I'm an important businessman. Important to them, that is, not important to you, I'm sure. Although I could be.'

'What business are you in?'

'Oh, I own a controlling interest in a small variety of industries. And a smaller interest in many more. Let's say I'm one of their investors.'

'And what have you invested in?'

'Government, of course. Their government. Or lack thereof.'

His accent was sometimes transatlantic, sometimes untraceable. I asked him where he was from.

'I have citizenship with a variety of nations.'

'But where were you born?'

'Ten-thousand metres up, on a flight between New York and Geneva. We were over water at the time.' He smiled. 'I am a citizen of nowhere, and therefore everywhere.'

'I see. Then where do you live?'

'I rotate between a variety of properties. Yourself?'

'I'm from Croydon, and I currently live in cramped University digs. I don't even have my own toilet.'

He raised his glass. 'And here you are drinking Dom Pérignon with the elite, you'll go far, my boy.'

'Thank you.' I raised my glass in return.

'And do you know why we're drinking Dom Pérignon and not vastly superior Ridgeview English sparkling wine?'

I smiled. 'Because these people have no fucking taste.'

We both laughed.

'Ben!'

I turned to see Amal, wearing a beautiful charcoal suit, and before I could extend my hand he was hugging me.

'Thank god you're here. I need you to rescue me.'

'From who?'

Before he could answer, the crowd had grown hushed as an older man in traditional white Arab dress with gold accoutrements entered from the corridor.

He stopped in front of Amal, who gave a courteous bow. 'Father.'

It was impossible to tell how old or how frail the man was; only his hands and face were visible. The hands were bony, but a healthy colour; and his face was full and round. He was a short, rotund man, with strong features, sharp dark eyes, and a thin goatee that looked painted on.

The eyes bored into Amal for just a beat, and then

he moved off towards the bar down the other end. Following behind him was an elderly woman in black and a younger woman in deep purple, both over six foot tall and with fierce crow-like faces.

'Mother, this is Ben, my friend,' he said to the older woman.

She did not even look at me. 'We have people for you to meet,' she told Amal instead.

'I know,' he sighed. He looked at the younger woman. 'I didn't know you were coming.'

'Why would you?' she asked, disappearing off.

'Don't leave,' he told me, 'I'll be right back.'

Half an hour passed, and still he had not fought his way back to me, so I began to wander through the crowd towards the bar. As I approached I could see two white leather sofas by a window, with Amal and his father seated on one, and a bald man in a grey suit opposite. Behind the bald man's sofa two other nondescript foreign men stood with arms folded, and behind Amal and his father, his mother and sister lingered like harpies. Amal was leant forward, trying to convince the bald man of something.

When he saw me his attention switched instantly. 'Ben! I'm so sorry.'

The break in attention seemed to be what the bald man had been waiting for. He got up immediately and began to shuffle out from the sofas, talking quickly but quietly with his men. The rest of the family watched him, both women as though desperate to say anything that would lure him back. He seemed to be getting away from them. Amal's attention was entirely on me. I was refilling my champagne glass.

'What do you want to drink?' I asked him.

This snapped the women's attention from the bald man onto me.

Without hesitation Amal laughed. 'Very funny, Ben, you know I don't drink.'

'Of course I know,' I lied.

He got up, pulling me away from the sofas. 'Come with me, there's someone I want you to meet.'

'Who is it?' I asked as he folded me through the crowd, but his attention was everywhere else. He was keeping an anxious watch around us.

He snatched my glass from my hand and dumped it on a table. 'This way, quickly!' Then he dragged me from the main room like a doll, into the corridor, pushing me into one of the small rooms. Without windows, it was almost pitch black. I saw his shadow move in front of me, and then a shaft of light peeked from the floor. He had lifted up the bottom of the canvas wall and was now slipping through the gap, his feet dangling in a void. Then he disappeared down out of sight.

'This way,' his voice echoed.

I looked around the tiny space, it was barely a changing room. After a beat, I knelt down, lifted up the canvas, dangled my legs through the hole, and disappeared into nothingness.

After a worrying second my feet landed on grass and my shoulder bumped on a scaffold pole. We were on the sloping bank of the river, underneath the constructed floor. He was sitting on one of the horizontal poles. I tested the sturdiness of another before I leant on it.

A moment's silence rang out between us. His eyes were closed. Water lapped at the shore. Wind rustled the pines. Birds cawed. And on top we could hear all the footsteps and the laughter and the drinking going on above our heads. Finally, one of us had to break the silence.

'You'll ruin your suit,' I told him.

'This costume?'

I raised an eyebrow. 'Is it a costume?'

'Oh yes. It says, "don't worry, we're not really Arabs, look,". And, of course, I'm the one that has to wear it, even when I'm not wearing a suit.'

Although he had snapped, his smile made it clear he was not angry at me.

He continued: 'It's the job of the other brother. My brother can be the straight arrow, the straight Arab: hard line, faithful. I can be the liberal one, the one Western businessmen can be photographed with.' He tilted his head back, looking up at the underneath of the floor. 'This is my life, the one I told you about; endless soirées. Schmoozing and networking with the rich and the powerful. Why not just put a sign on me that says, "please buy our oil, also we'll stop chopping off hands."'

'It doesn't seem so bad.'

'Even the taste of champagne can sour.' He looked back down, at his feet now. 'I thought I'd get a few more years of freedom, but my father is far more ill than anyone outside the family knows. He won't last another year.'

The cold lake mist had encroached further now, the air around us damp and chilled.

'Will your brother be a good king?'

'He's my father's heir. The world won't even notice; they'll just think he's looking well again.'

Clacking footsteps echoed above us on the floor of one of the side rooms. We listened.

'Where *is* the little shit?' a woman seethed.

Amal held a finger to his lips, then mouthed the words "*my sister*".

'He had *one* job!' she groaned.

His mother's voice machine-gunned some aggressive Arabic. The sister shot back. I watched his intense concentration.

The rat-a-tat conversation went on for a minute or two. Then Amal whispered:

'They're talking about you now.'

'Anything good?' I asked.

He just smiled.

'At least your father doesn't bitch about you behind your back.'

'He's the worst of them.' The smile had dropped from his face. 'Sometimes I'm horrified to think I'm his son.'

I did not comment.

'He has so much power, and he does nothing but hold onto it. Like money in the bank. Never spending it, never giving it away; it just sits there, doing nothing but accumulating interest. That's the real difference between me and my brother: he wouldn't do *a thing* differently.'

There was a scream from above us. It sounded like his mother. Then she shouted something in Arabic. There were footsteps running, rushing, amongst the screamed words was Amal's name.

He jumped up to the hole and began to scramble back through. I went to follow him, but he held out his hand to stop me.

'No, you'd better go round the side.'

I watched his feet disappear and then ducked my way through the web of steel before I emerged onto the grass and circled back to the ramp where I had entered.

Guests were spilling down it, I had to swim upstream to make it back into the tent.

The place was boiling with energy. People were shouting over each other, several barking into satellite phones. A handful were talking calmly and finishing their drinks. The family were nowhere to be seen.

The exceedingly calm man I had shared the view with earlier was still exceedingly calm, still seated in the same position. I sat on a different sofa and stared out into the mist that was now all encompassing.

Within five minutes the sky was swarming with helicopters.

It was four hours before I saw Amal again. I was alone now, it was dark, and all I could see in the windows was the ghost of my own face. He drifted into the reflection.

'Ben, you're still here.'

'I didn't know how to get home,' I told him, turning, 'I can't click my fingers and make a helicopter appear.'

'All you needed to do was ask one of the staff.'

I gave a gentle smile. 'And I wanted to make sure you were ok.'

He looked ten years older. Pale, eyes bloodshot; he had been crying. I had heard a lot of wailing, but that had not been him.

'What's happened?' I asked.

'My brother, he's been in an accident—car accident.'

'Is he ok?'

'No. No, he's not ok.' He took a deep breath. I got the impression he was trying not to throw up. 'They're going to keep him on life support until my parents can see him. They're in the air now.'

He rubbed his eyes, then perched on a sofa. He was as stiff as a mannequin. I perched too.

'I have to go,' he whispered.

'Of course.'

'Will you come with me?'

I didn't answer.

He dug his fingers into his temples. 'Fuck, fuck, fuck. My brother is dead. All but dead. And all I keep thinking is *why did he have to do this to me?*'

I made no sound.

'When I was a child I used to fantasise about just this. When I grew up I realised it was a curse. Then I ran as far as my leash would stretch. Not very far, it turned out.' He gave another of those despairing smiles.

I trod carefully. 'Did you mean what you said... earlier? That you would do things differently.'

His eyes met mine for second, reading them. 'Yes.'

'Then... I don't mean to be insensitive... but things being as they are, maybe this is a chance.'

'A chance for what?'

'I think you're a better man than you know. Maybe

you could do some good.'

He pondered for a second, the black cloud momentarily lifted. 'I can't do it alone. Will you come with me?'

Again, I didn't answer. I felt the fear of new things come over me. 'As what?' was the best defence I could put up.

'A friend,' he shrugged. 'No, as an advisor.'

'I—'

'We'll pay you. Fifty thousand a year.'

I went to speak again. 'I don't—'

'Seventy thousand. And when I don't need you anymore, you can come back to Britain an experienced diplomatic player. You'll be able to walk into a job in the Foreign Office. Or if you really want to be an MP, your party will be clamouring to have you as a junior minister.'

It all sounded attractive, but I had to tell the truth: 'I don't think I'll be much use to you.'

'I think you're a more useful man than you know,' he said with a little smile, turning my phrase back on me. 'Maybe together *we* could do some good.'

'I don't know,' I told him.

He sighed. 'Come with me, don't come with me, it's entirely up to you. But my helicopter leaves in four minutes.'

3

An Antique Land

WE MAY HAVE LEFT on the same helicopter, but we ended up on different planes. Seven hours later, as the jet banked and the dawn kissed the city, I got my first glimpse of his kingdom. Blue sea shimmered to the right, endless desert rose and fell in dunes to the left. In the middle, grids of whitewashed houses began to glow in the sun, and from a small pocket of green grass and trees, skyscrapers reached up towards us.

I landed on a foreign planet, following a team of suits who led me through the drowning sea of heat between the airport terminal and the air-conditioned car.

From the car I saw the sun shining like a beacon off the tips of glass towers, but we turned away from them, away from the city, and towards a small gated community of large cream buildings. The car pulled up in front of one the size of a small hotel, and I was ushered inside into the cool. Fans whirred from every ceiling, above the heads of a smiling staff.

It was all mine. The staff were all mine too. Nine rooms, a cook, a valet, two maids, a gardener, two footmen, a driver, and a butler and housekeeper to supervise them. The butler showed me to an enormous and lavishly decorated bedroom with a balcony over the modest green garden.

Waiting in the dressing room was a tailor, who took my measurements and assured me I would have ten suits in three days. He apologised that for now I would have to make do with the off-the-peg options in the wardrobe. They were all designer, down to the socks.

I spent that first day having conversations with the butler and housekeeper about how I liked things done. What did I want for breakfast? What time? Where would I prefer to eat? Lunch. Dinner. Supper. Were there any English foods I would like imported? Any plants I preferred in the garden? And lastly, if there was anything about the house I was unhappy with. I asked how that could be possible.

I was informed that this gated community, whatever it was, had three swimming pools that could be booked for private use, as well as tennis courts, and a squash court. Alcohol was allowed, would I like a drink now? With dinner?

The only thing I asked for that day was a fast internet connection and a laptop. After two days I asked for British television, they gave me everything Sky offers.

Amal did not visit until the third day. I had spent the first two swimming and reading as much about the country as I could find. That meant its Wikipedia entry and the little I could find reported on British and American news websites.

'Has no one told you anything?' Amal almost shouted.

'No.'

'No one has been to see you?'

I shook my head.

He huffed in disbelief. Disbelief and anger. He was pacing. 'Abderrazzaq!'

The butler appeared. 'Yes, sir?'

'Get Daniel al-Hadi down here now. No excuses. If he's not here in the next hour he'll have to answer to me.'

'Very good, your Royal Highness.' He nodded and disappeared at speed.

He stopped pacing, looking out over the garden where the sprinklers *phut-phutting* an arc of water had made a glistening rainbow.

'They switched off the life support yesterday. I've been officially declared the heir to the throne.'

'Do I say congratulations?'

'No one knows what to say. Mostly they just nod, but even then they don't know what face to pull.'

A minute later the butler returned. 'Your Royal Highness.'

'Yes?'

'His office says he's already on his way.'

'I'm sure they do. Thank you, Abderrazzaq.'

'Thank you, your Royal Highness.' He bowed and left.

'Is that how I should address you?' I asked.

'Please don't.'

He came from the window and, as was his habit, perched on the arm of a sofa.

'Who is this Daniel al-Hadi?' I asked him.

'Daniel is the head of Government Operations. The civil service, I suppose. Every week he holds an audience with my father, along with the heads of the military, and anyone else that my father or Daniel decide is appropriate, depending on the events of the week: ambassadors, experts, heads of department.'

'Like a cabinet meeting.'

'Somewhat. It is Daniel's job to enact the will of my father, as decreed at these audiences. He is the lever by which my father turns the wheels of government.'

'Like the Cabinet Secretary.'

'Yes. And like the Cabinet Secretary he provides advice. Except Daniel's advice is always the same: keep things as they are, do things as we have always done them.'

'Like the Cabinet Secretary.'

'He puts it in a variety of ways, uses a variety of terms: continuity, consistency, tradition, heritage, certainty, security; but it all amounts to the same thing. He hates change. He'll *despise* you.'

Twenty minutes later the low rumble of a big black car announced a visitor. Daniel al-Hadi glided into the room at such speed but with such grace I thought for a second he was riding a Segway. He was an average sized man in a charcoal three-piece suit and striped plum tie. Every accoutrement was present: tie pin, watch chain, lapel pin, cufflinks, rings, but all silver; he passed for modest by the standards of recent company. He had grey hair and eyebrows that looked like thick dust. Beyond that he was as smooth, impenetrable, and impossible to grasp as cigar smoke.

'Your Royal Highness,' he purred in perfect received pronunciation, 'and Mr Hollow, what a pleasure to meet you.' He shook my hand earnestly.

He had in tow two younger men, each carrying leather-bound books as large as Atlases in piles so high they could not see where they stepped. He gestured to the large dining table at the other end of the room. They laid the books side by side, covering almost the entire surface.

'Before we get into anything else, I thought it would be a good idea to provide you with as much information as possible: we have a wide variety of texts to get you up to speed. History, economy, geography, *geology*; by the time you have read them you will know more about our country than even myself. We have also arranged for the authors of these volumes to meet with you, starting—shall we say—from a fortnight's time? That way you will be able to ask them any questions you have.'

I ran my fingers over the red leather of the nearest tome: The Political and Economic History of Argolis, 1947–1986: Volume I.

'You expect him to get through all this in a fortnight?' Amal asked.

'I know it seems daunting, your Royal Highness, but Mr Hollow and I went to the same college, I know what we're made of.' He puffed up his chest with pride.

'I understand that audiences with my father will not resume until next week.'

'That is correct, and you will be there, of course.'

'As will Ben.'

He frowned, about to speak, but Amal got in first:

'He is my chief advisor.'

'Of course, your Royal Highness, but perhaps it would be best for Mr Hollow to finish his study first.'

'No, he's coming.'

'I really think that in order for Mr Hollow to give you the best advice he must—'

'He's coming, Daniel. That's my final decision.'

He was silent for a beat. 'Very good.' He turned to me. 'These men are your personal secretaries—'

'I have already arranged Ben's staff,' Amal interrupted.

Daniel hid his genuine reaction with a smile. 'I see, then perhaps these men could operate as liaison to Government Operations—'

'That won't be necessary: Ben's role is an advisory one, he won't be drafting papers or commissioning reports, these secretaries will be of no use.'

'They can supplement—'

'There's no need to waste your resources.'

'There will be no waste, they have already been assigned—'

'Then un-assign them.'

There was another silent beat. 'I'm sure your Royal Highness would not want to see these men out of a job.'

'They will not be working for Mr Hollow, is that clear?'

'Quite clear. Thank you, your Royal Highness.'

He swivelled on his heel towards me, the two men fell in behind.

'Mr Hollow, are there any questions you have of me?'

I thought for a second. 'Not at the moment.'

'Very well.' He started to turn.

'But I'm sure I will have some. How should I get in touch?'

'Your staff will be able to contact anyone you need through the central government switchboard.'

'Thank you.'

He nodded to me, turned, 'Highness,' nodded to Amal, and marched briskly out the door, the two men in formation behind.

✦

For thousands of years, the area around Argolis contained only a few small fishing communities. They lived in isolation, content with their simple lives. They were visited by the Prophet after the conquest of Mecca, during his final years, and converted to Islam. This led to greater prosperity as Allah smiled on them, and soon the seas were filled with pearl oysters.

In the 19th century the communities were invaded and subjugated by the British Army. They enslaved the fishermen and exploited their pearl catches to prop up their failing empire.

In 1945, Abdullah, the humble son of a fisherman,

formed a militia with other men from the coastal communi-
ties, and by 1947 they had overthrown the British
oppressors, who retreated, never to be seen in this land again.

The Ancient History of Argolis for Boys (school text-
book)

Artefacts uncovered in the area surrounding mod-
ern-day Argolis show a long history of human
habitation and regional trade including with Mesopo-
tamia. The area was settled by several tribes along
the coast and was Islamised in the seventh century.

Many incursions and bloody battles took place
along the coast when the Portuguese invaded the
area. Conflicts between the maritime communities
and the British led to the sacking of the small fishing
communities by British forces in 1812 and again in
1820, which resulted in the first of several British
treaties with the tribal rulers in 1821. These treaties
led to peace and prosperity along the coast which
lasted until the 1930s, when the pearl trade collapsed, leading to significant hardship among the
coastal communities.

In 1947, Britain decided to withdraw from its involvement in the area; this allowed the head of the
military, General Abdullah, to seize control of the
coastal communities.

en.wikipedia.org/wiki/Argolis#History#Pre-1947

Following the defeat of the British forces, the coastal communities formed a single kingdom, taking as its name that of their liberator, Abdullah bin-Argolis, whom they declared their king. Allah was pleased with Abdullah's leadership and blessed his people with vast underground lakes of oil. The revenues provided for military protection against aggressive neighbours, and had the ability to tame and control the new and dangerous superpower of America.

Unlike the Imperial oppressors of the past, King Abdullah shared his wealth with the people, leading to huge development in education and infrastructure. However, this led to mass immigration as peoples from all parts of the world came to exploit the safety and prosperity of Argolis.

Omar bin-Saad al-Albahr, The Political and Economic History of Argolis, 1947–1986: Volume I

General Abdullah consolidated the coastal communities into a unified nation, declaring himself king in 1948, taking the name Abdullah bin-Argolis. The new kingdom was initially reliant on limited agriculture and fishing revenues.

In 1950, vast reserves of oil were discovered in the western desert region, and full-scale development of the oil fields began in 1951 under the US-controlled Argamoil (Argolisian American Oil Company). Oil provided Argolis with economic prosperity and substantial political leverage in the Gulf.

Cultural life rapidly developed, primarily in the Al-bahr community, which became the business and commercial district when the communities were consolidated into a single city-state. However, the large influx of foreign workers in the oil industry increased pre-existing xenophobia. At the same time, the government became increasingly wasteful and extravagant. By the 1960s this had led to large governmental deficits and excessive foreign borrowing.

The vast wealth generated by oil revenues was beginning to have an even greater impact on Argolisian society. It led to rapid technological (but not cultural) modernisation, urbanization, mass public education and the creation of new media. Although there was dramatic change in the social and economic life of the country, political power continued to be monopolized by the royal family leading to discontent among many Argolisians who began to look for wider participation in government.

en.wikipedia.org/wiki/Argolis#History#The_Founding_of_Argolis

The king and his wife, Cythna, had six sons; the eldest of which he gave his own name, Abdullah.

A Historical Guide to Argolis (tourist information guide)

Between 1938–1960 King Abdullah and his wife Cythna produced nine sons: Khalid, Faisal, Fahd, Abdullah, Sultan, Talal, Nayef, Muqrin, and Salman.

Between 1964 and 1973 King Abdullah's three eldest sons were murdered; Khalid and Faisal by staff in their own households, and Fahd by his wife.

en.wikipedia.org/wiki/Argolis#History#The_Rise_of_the_Heir

In 1975, al-Abu was carried to heaven. He was succeed [sic] by his eldest son, Abdullah. When Abdullah left Argolis to attend a royal visit to Qatar, Sultan, along with two other brothers: Talal and Salman, attempted to seize control of the kingdom. They murdered the other brothers, Nayef and Muqrin, out of paranoia and fear that they could betray them as they had betrayed Abdullah.

When Abdullah returned, he reconquered the royal palace, defeating Sultan single-handed in the battle. Talal confessed to his crimes and was beheaded following the law of the kingdom that he himself had once believed in. But Abdullah took pity on his youngest brother, Salman, who was of simple mind, and decreed that he would live in comfortable isolation in his home with his wives. He died peacefully, of a stroke, in 1986. The people of Argolis celebrated for ten days to mark their gratitude at the king's return and mercy.

The king's reign led to a further increase in the economic prosperity initiated by his father, and a continued strict observance of the Prophet's teachings maintained the bountiful happiness of Argolis.

Ali ibn-Muhammad, Argolis in Context - For English Speakers

King Abdullah bin-Argolis died of a suspected stroke in 1975. He was succeeded by his son, Abdullah bin-Abdullah, who took the al-Argolis name as his father had done. From this point, the first King Abdullah al-Argolis has been affectionately referred to as "al-Abu", the father. (After her death in 1982, Cythna was officially declared on her tomb as Cythna al-Argolis, and since affectionately referred to as "al-Umm", the mother, although this is less commonly used.)

In 1976, King Abdullah II's younger brother, Sultan, attempted to seize power whilst Abdullah was abroad. Upon his return three days later, Abdullah ordered a military assault on the royal palaces that left thirty-seven dead, including Sultan, Nayef, and Muqrin. Talal was executed the next week following a show trial. Salman, the youngest, was sentenced to life under house-arrest. He hanged himself in his bathroom in 1980.

In 1977, Argolis gained 35% control in Argamoil, thereby decreasing US control over Argolisian oil.

Due to regional instability, oil prices quadrupled in the 1980s.

Abdullah bin-Abdullah's reign saw economic and social development stagnate. Pressure increased on the government to allow more democratic involvement leading to student demonstrations in the Albahr district. At a similar time, other forces seized control of the airport, holding hostage an Egyptian Airlines flight. The militants involved were in part angered by what they considered to be the corruption and un-Islamic nature of the government. The government regained control of the airport after 6 days and those captured were executed. Part of the response of the royal family was to enforce a much stricter observance of traditional religious and social norms in the country (for example, the closure of cinemas) and to roll back some of the economic reforms instituted by King Abdullah I.

en.wikipedia.org/wiki/Argolis#History#King_Abdullah_II

After some years of hardship, caused by immigrant rebels from neighbouring countries, a new era dawned on Argolis in 1987, with the birth of Iman bin-Abdullah bin-Abdullah, heir to the throne. The king was blessed again in 1992, with a second son, Amal.

This new era led to greater trade with Western nations,

who finally began to look on Argolis as a superior nation and system of government. In 2001, to further share the bounties of his leadership, and to educate the people in government, the King instituted the system of Royal Audiences where ordinary people's concerns would be raised with the king, so as to continue to better the lives of the country's citizens.

The Modern History of Argolis for Boys (school text-book)

In 1987 King Abdullah II declared a new era upon the birth of his son, Iman, with his wife Fatuwah bint-Muhammad. In 1989, their daughter, Rania, was born. And in 1992, another son, Amal.

In 1988, Argolis bought out the American interests in Argamoil, renaming the company ArgOil; however, Abdullah continued to develop close relations with the United States and increased the purchase of American and European military equipment.

Argolis' relations with the West began to cause growing concern among some of the ulama (guardians of Islamic doctrine) and students of sharia law, and was one of the issues that led to an increase in Islamist terrorism in the country, as well as Islamist terrorist attacks in Western countries by Argolisian nationals.

Islamism was not the only source of hostility to the government. Although now extremely wealthy, Argolis' economy was near stagnant. High taxes and a growth in unemployment have contributed to discontent, and has been reflected in a rise in civil unrest, and discontent with the royal family. In response, a number of limited 'reforms' were initiated by King Abdullah. In April 2000, he introduced the 'First Law', which emphasised the duties and responsibilities of a ruler. In December 2000, the royal 'audiences' were officially declared a process of government and required by law. The King's intent was to respond to dissent while making as few actual changes in the status quo as possible.[citation needed] Abdullah made it clear that he did not have democracy in mind: 'A system based on elections is not consistent with our Islamic creed, which [approves of] government by consultation [shūrā].'

en.wikipedia.org/wiki/Argolis#History#A_New_Era

Argolis is economically prosperous, safe, secure from the hostile nations of Iran and Israel, free from terrorism, and moving towards a carbon-neutral future. We owe this to our unique system of government, and to my father.

Speech given in 2012 to the UN General Assembly by
Iman bin-Abdullah bin-Abdullah

*In 2018, Iman bin-Abdullah bin-Abdullah died, aged 31, when his Ferrari collided with a tree. His brother Amal, succeeded him as heir.

Note at the bottom of the Argolis Wikipedia page

✦

When my eyes stung from reading and the world had turned dark, I retired to the bedroom, and to the balcony. Over the soft white shapes of the complex I could just see the lights of the city, miles away. All I could hear was foreign music on the warm desert wind, and the voice in my head that echoed, *you're a long way from home, you're a long way from home,* and it was *so* wonderful.

Part II

... Near them, on the sand,
Half sunk a shattered visage lies, whose frown,
And wrinkled lip, and sneer of cold command,
Tell that its sculptor well those passions read
Which yet survive, stamped on these lifeless things,
The hand that mocked them, and the heart that fed;

Ozymandias, Percy Bysshe Shelley

4

On the Pedestal

Us INVITED MEN, and a thousand more, stood before the body wrapped in a simple cotton shroud. They said prayers I did not understand, but did not need to. The body was carried to a hot, stony graveyard, the pale dirt speckled with mourners. Amal placed him in his shallow grave, laid on his side to face Mecca, and we watched as he alone piled the earth around him until the spot was just another lump among thousands. One by one we placed a white stone on the pile, and lastly Amal's father placed the humble marker by his head. It was not the funeral of a prince.

The wake was something else.

The royal palace was everything you would imagine. From the outside it was an enormous sandstone castle, the battlements patrolled by men with rifles; the only windows tiny triangular pockmarks. Inside, the lack of windows lent the place a cavernous, subterranean atmosphere; disconnected from the city.

The main hall was three storeys high. Gold, in intricate geometric patterns, climbed its way up whitewashed columns that flanked the walls and formed alcoves on three sides. Above the centre, three pyramidal chandeliers illuminated a sea of low chairs and sofas. A buffet table ran along one side, and in another room a bar was set up for Western guests. The lighting was soft, with pockets of shadow, tricking your hypothalamus out of any sense of time. It was an atmosphere that could be enchanting one moment, and disorientating the next.

In every hall and room throngs of well-dressed mourners with nothing but a passing connection to the deceased flitted in and out of sight like falling glitter. Trays of oranges, melons, olives and dates became skins and stones. Legs of cured meat were transformed into stripped bones. Towers of flatbreads vanished entirely. Every few minutes a piercing laugh would cut through the revels, and each time shed a little more decorum from the atmosphere.

'Who are you?' A bulbous American demanded of me when I asked if he was queuing for the buffet. He wore a fawn suit that only exaggerated his considerable width, and his long red tie was tucked into his belt.

'Ben Hollow,' I told him.

'I don't want your fucking name. Who are you?'

'I'm an advisor.'

He scoffed as though I might have said I was twelve years old. 'I'm an important man, I own a company. I build things, have you ever built anything?'

'I asked if this was the queue for the buffet.'

He huffed, I had not got his point, and waddled away.

I lingered by the buffet table, not knowing anyone in sight, and not seeing anyone who needed a new friend. As a shoal of silver guests scattered with their food, I narrowly avoided collision with a young blonde man in a sharp blue suit making his way through the food in the opposite direction.

'Sorry,' I apologised.

'Ah!' he exclaimed, adding 'a fellow Brit,' in a fairly thick Scottish accent.

'Yes,' I smiled.

'Mark,' he held out a hand, 'Mark Lowden.'

'Ben,' I said as I shook it.

He was a handsome man. Sharp-jawed and athletic, nothing like me.

'What do you do, Ben?'

'I'm an... friend of the family.'

'I see. Did you know Iman well?'

'No. You?'

'I only met him once.'

'What do you do?'

'I work for a company that works with ArgOil. We do geological surveys.'

I smiled, trying to think of a new question to ask him which was not tedious, but he moved the conversation along himself:

'How long are you going to be in the country?'

'Indefinitely.'

'Really? Well then, I and a few friends from the embassy have a party every now and then, we call it an "empire party", which is a bit distasteful. You should come. What we do is we have tea, and British food, and we watch a football match, or Antiques Roadshow or something else. If you're missing home, it's a nice tonic; which is something we also have. You'd be surprised what the taste of Marmite or the sound of Fiona Bruce will do to you after a month here.'

I smiled politely and told him I would come if I got the chance.

As I moved around the palace further, stepping over the sparkling carpet, trying not to crunch on the lost earrings, I passed a quartet of inaudible musicians, then the bar, where energetic white people shouted and screeched, spilling champagne that ran off the glass top. Corks popped and ice clinked. In corners by beautifully mathematical mosaics and gaping clay urns, guests snapped smiling selfies and debated which Instagram filter to apply. At first the place had been teeming with staff, but now all those not on the bar had retreated to safer quarters, waiting out the storm.

Down a quiet corridor there was a library, and sitting alone beneath the two-storey towers of books, was my leather-faced new friend from the Loch Ness party. He still had a glass of whisky moulded to his hand, but this time a book in his lap. In here the sounds of partying were a gentle rumble.

'Hello, again,' I announced in a hushed voice.

He glanced up from his reading, then a broad smile cracked his face. 'My boy!'

I smiled back, then his face turned from joy to admiration.

'Look at you, you do work fast. Would you like a job?'

'With you?'

'Absolutely. I can always use a fast worker.'

'I already have one, I think.'

He nodded slowly. 'That's right, I've heard.'

'You have?'

'I heard that the prince had a new advisor, a young Jewish man.'

'I'm not Jewish.' I must have frowned.

'You're in Arabia, if your grandmother ever ate a

pickle, you're Jewish.'

'I'll keep that in mind.'

He nodded, before adding with a wink, 'The room you're looking for is through there,' pointing to a door opposite.

'Thanks.'

I moved out and across the hallway, reaching my hand out to turn the doorknob. As I did, it was wrenched inwards and I instinctively flitted to the side, hiding against the next door.

'HELP!?' a voice screamed, but not in desperation, in disbelief. 'He *can't* do the job, mother.' It was Amal's sister, Rania.

'What would you have me do?' came the croaked reply.

'Declare me the heir.'

'Your brother is popular with the students, the rebels, immigrants, not to mention the West; he may be good for us. *All* of us.'

'Students and immigrants don't run this country, the ulama do.'

'*Your father* runs this country,' her mother spat.

'Not for much longer!' She slammed the door.

She stood huffing, leaning with her hand on the knob. I did not even breathe, but suddenly she straightened, and turned. There was a split second when her fierce eyes bore into me, then they drifted to something more interesting. Such as the air around me.

'Oh, it's you,' she sighed. 'Where did you come from?'

I took a second to find my voice, we had never spoken before, and she inspired fear like a severe teacher. 'I was just in the library.'

'You know that's not what I meant. Amal never mentioned you, not once, and then suddenly it's "Ben, Ben, Ben..." What is it he sees in you? More than just friends, surely.'

'An ally, perhaps.'

'*We* are his allies!'

She craned her head up higher than mine, tilting it down like a heron above the water. It took all my will not to step back. 'Maybe he doesn't see it that way,' I croaked.

She snorted, straightening her clothes.

'But if I'm his ally,' I started, 'and you're his ally, doesn't that make *us* allies?'

This time she laughed in my face.

'I know you're suspicious of me, I would be too,' I said, trying to be genuine. 'The truth is I don't know what he sees in me.' I offered a pathetic smile, she did not return it.

'You've worked your way in, you...' she faltered, 'what is that animal?' She thought for a second.

I tried to help her: 'Worm?'

Her eyes snapped but she didn't respond, still thinking.

'Snake?'

'Cuckoo,' she growled.

I gave a self-pitying smile, never having had such malign motives assigned to me. 'I'm just another underqualified, overpaid advisor. I've already made it in politics.'

She had started to leave, but now she turned. 'Well then, advisor. What would you advise my brother do about me?'

I tried to see past her talons and beak. 'You're a very strong person. You care about your family. You deserve respect.'

'Deserve!?' She marched on me now. 'I'll tell you what I deserve. I could be a new Cleopatra. If I had a penis I would be the heir!'

'I agree,' I said with a smirk, 'it's a terrible system.'

She stopped on my smile. 'Why do you say it that way?'

I tried to cover my tracks. 'No reason.'

'The monarchy has kept my family safe for seventy years.'

'You're defending a system that has kept you from what you want because of the way you were born.'

'Don't try and pour democracy in my ear, Jew.' She leant in and whispered in mine: 'I know what you want.'

She straightened up, listening. The rumble of the party had been silenced.

She whipped round in a flurry of purple and gold, and marched down the corridor, calling: 'Maybe I'll give it to you!'

I followed her at a clip, having to skip every few steps to keep up. The main hall was silent, every guest standing at attention. Amal had arrived and even the most raucous drunkards were staring at him with gently bowed heads. He nodded to them all in a respectful, if slightly shy, style.

Out of the crowd Rania emerged, moving at speed towards him.

'Sister,' he said with respect.

On course for the exit, she ploughed her shoulder into his, knocking him off balance. The crowd gasped.

The champagne ran out at ten. The last guests left at ten fourteen. I found Amal sitting in the middle of the sea of sofas, under the now dimmed pyramids.

I sat a couple of sofas away, he looked lost and I did not want to break into his thoughts. He had managed the funeral with fantastic grace, I could not believe he was so affected by his sister's antics.

After some minutes he whispered, 'You don't see the body, do you, in England?'

I was startled by the break in the silence. 'No, not generally. Some do, but mostly it's a closed coffin.'

'Why do you think that is? The Vikings watched them burn, Jews sit Shiva. But the British, you just hide them away in a box and bury them.'

'Actually, it's mostly cremations now.'

'Why?'

'It's more practical.'

He smirked. 'See what I mean?'

I shrugged. 'I guess we don't see the point: they're dead.'

His head went down. Unable to make eye contact any more, I moved quietly to the chair opposite him. What came next trickled out a few drops at a time:

'In our tradition, male relatives wash the body before it is wrapped in a shroud. My brother only had my father and me. I had to do it alone. They had to "mend" the body after the crash. The first part they did in the hospital morgue, before they could move him. I spoke to the doctor, he told me Iman's blood contained alcohol. Large amounts. He was so drunk it was no surprise he couldn't control the car. My parents have made sure that it won't be in the coroner's report. Once again, my father gets to write history how he wants it.'

'What harm can it do now?' I asked gently.

'When I was fifteen, I was sent on some bullshit inter-faith bridge-building sojourn, hardly different from the stuff they send me on now. It was to the Vatican, and I smuggled back a bottle of wine in the diplomatic bag. I was so stupid; it was communion wine. It tasted like vinegar. The servants found it, of course, in my room. My parents went crazy, I don't know what was worse: the thought that I had drunk alcohol, or that I might be a Christian. My brother told them it was his. They were so disappointed. But this was my brother, so they soon got over it. He told me that if I ever did it again, he would kill me himself.'

He looked up into my eyes, I could see the glowing pyramids in his.

'Someone murdered him.'

I swallowed.

'And they did it in such a brilliant way that the murder weapon would be redacted from the medical reports. No one will dare poke at it any further. And if they do smell a cover up, they'll find out he had alcohol in his blood and that will explain it. It's the perfect murder.'

We sat in silence for some minutes as I turned everything over in my mind. It took me some time, not being particularly well acquainted with murder. At last, I whispered almost to myself, 'Assassination.'

'What?'

'Could it be an assassination? They killed the heir to the throne.'

This seemed to be something he had not considered. A look of horror crossed his face as he spoke: 'I could be next.'

I thought for a few moments longer, my mind still unlocking new possibilities. 'Or...' I started, 'which might even be scarier; the person who did it *wants you* to become king.'

This possibility did not seem to register with him like the first.

'Oh, Ben,' he simply whimpered, holding my hand, 'you're the only one I can trust.'

5

The Heart That Fed

THE ROYAL AUDIENCES recommenced following ten official days of mourning; and so I attended my first at ten o'clock on a—by now unsurprisingly—scorching Tuesday morning. I was ferried for the second time to the royal palace, glimpsing through the tinted windows of the car dirt streets leading off the tarmacked boulevards we cruised down. We passed fellow Range Rovers, Mercedes, Lamborghinis, and Ferrari's, but down these dirt streets I saw flashes of real life: dogs yapping, children selling fruit, mothers hanging out of windows, men walking, laughing, others with heads down, sand in their eyes.

Upon arrival I was ushered into a gilded room. On a dais sat an empty wooden throne, startling in its modesty, and behind it a velvet curtain. Ten metres away were eight gilded chairs, facing the throne in a perfect arc, except for one, which was set just one chair length further back: my chair. Daniel al-Hadi's hand had just lifted off it when I entered. He floated out of a different door.

Standing behind the chairs, in a tight group, were three old, but not elderly, men in different military uniforms. One khaki, one blue, one green. They were whispering intensely, but each regarded my entrance with nothing more than a glance. The one in khaki studied Daniel's exit before his glance came.

At the other end of the room was a table covered with pitta bread, olives, tomatoes, hummus, ful (fava bean hummus), falafel, za'atar (dried herbs and sesame seed dip), dukkah (herbs, nuts, and spice mix dip), labneh (yogurt cheese, somewhere between ricotta and mozzarella), nabulsi cheese (somewhat like halloumi), and gallons of olive oil. Always having a healthy appetite, I dived in. As I was pouring myself a long, cardamom-scented cup of coffee, the khaki man broke off from his group and began to fill a plate for himself.

He wore thin stubble but a thick moustache, I recognised that moustache from my reading as belonging to General Othman bin-Tal, head of the army. I presumed the blue and green men were his counterparts in the navy and air force.

'You must be His Highness's new advisor: Mr Hollow,' he said without his eyes leaving the food he was spooning. 'Benjamin.'

'Benedict, actually.'

He looked at me now, frowning with disappointment at his mistake, looking at me as though *I* might be the one mistaken. But then it went, and he smiled thinly. '*Benedict*. I'm sorry, Mr Hollow.'

He was a shorter man than me, with a face that crumpled near his neck like a bullmastiff. He had a rough, uncivilised look, and a gruff way of moving, I could tell instantly that he and Daniel did not get on, and could tell why.

'Ben will do,' I told him.

'Not here. Here you're Mr Hollow, don't deny yourself the only respect they'll show you.'

'On the contrary, by surrendering it voluntarily they can't deliberately demean me.'

He shook his head. 'That's the wrong tactic, if you don't mind me saying. In war it's always the same, where you're strong make yourself look weak, and where you're weak make yourself look strong. You're new, you're an outsider, they won't respect you, so make sure it looks to everyone else like they *do*. Believe me, I know: I wasn't born in the Albahr district like Daniel, and I didn't go to the university either. Raised in a poor fishing village I even spoke a different dialect, I had to earn their respect the hard way.'

I smiled genuinely. 'Thanks for the advice.'

'You're welcome.' He stood with his plate now, ready to rejoin his colleagues.

'You didn't tell me your name.'

'Othman, I'm in charge of our little army, but my colleagues here are Admiral of the Fleet and Marshal of the Air Force, far more important.'

'There you go using that tactic on me now, General.'

He raised an eyebrow.

'The admiral has two ships, some small patrol boats, and no more than seven hundred sailors. The marshal has twelve planes, and as many helicopters, less than five hundred men, half of them engineers. But there are ten thousand men in your army. You have twenty British-built tanks. In fact, if my maths is correct, given that around three quarters of those living in Argolis are migrants, you command one out of every twenty-five citizens. Factor out women and children and it must be closer to one in ten men.'

His face did not change, except the eyebrow returned to rest. 'Actually, my tanks are French. The marshal's planes are British. The Hawks, to be precise. The rest are Italian, American...' He paused before adding, 'I think you will serve His Highness very well. But...' he did not smile, 'you really should have let me think I'd fooled you.'

He returned to his group.

Just as I had finished eating, the military men suddenly snapped to attention. I looked up to see the king had entered through the curtain, Amal at his side. Everyone bowed, I tried to catch up, jerking violently. The king took to his throne, everyone else moved to their seats. I slipped into mine next to Amal's, and in the process of sitting down pulled it forward into line with the others. I glanced around, looking for Daniel: he had appeared on a stool by the throne, on the right hand of the king, eyes on mine, with a badly disguised frown.

Sitting in the eight chairs facing them were Amal, me; the general, admiral, and marshal; and three other men, who had arrived just in time, I neither recognised nor had been introduced to.

After some initial pleasantries and welcomes, Daniel got down to business: 'The pressing issue of today is of course the eight terrorists that were captured in the Albahr district yesterday morning, as I am sure you will all be aware.'

I was not. I was sure it had not been in the English-language newspaper, and had not seen it online. I had no doubt it was buried in the mountains of documents that arrived at my house every day.

The king whispered something we could not hear, Daniel leaned in to pick it up. He then directed a question to one of the men I did not know:

'How were these men able to enter the Albahr district? You were supposed to have tightened security.'

The man wore a black uniform, was rather fat, and quite flustered. 'We did, we did. But half the people working in that district are migrants, they don't have papers to carry.'

'I am right in thinking that we have not abandoned the work permit system? I certainly was not aware that we had.'

'Of course not.'

'So they must all have permits.'

'In theory.'

'In theory?' Daniel's eyebrows raised, as though his innocent interest was piqued.

'What I mean is... is that it is simply not possible for us to check everyone who enters and leaves that area. It is the most densely populated area of the city.'

'Why not?'

The fat man looked politely incredulous. 'We don't have the men.'

'Then take them from somewhere else.'

'We're already spread too thin across the rest of the city as it is.'

'Then you must make better use of your resources.'

'But—'

'If I might interrupt?' spoke the general.

'Of course,' Daniel purred.

The fat man, who I now gathered was chief of the police, nodded earnestly, looking for help.

'I have two-thousand men currently barracked one mile outside the city with nothing to do but drive their officers mad. I would be happy to offer them to Waa'il to assist with security inside the city.'

Daniel leant in to hear the king's opinion, before pronouncing: 'Very well, sort it out between the two of you. The pressing matter is whether we execute these men in al-Abu Square.'

'What?' It escaped me before I had a chance to stop myself.

Everyone looked at me, but especially Daniel. He might have licked his lips.

'Yes, Mr Hollow. That is what we need to discuss. If you would rather remove yourself, I'm sure—'

'Not at all,' I stated confidently.

'I say yes,' announced the general, 'public beheading in al-Abu Square, as always, we cannot show weakness, especially now.'

The admiral and marshal nodded.

'You're not going to behead these people!?' I blurted.

'Mr Hollow,' Daniel admonished me, 'may I remind you that you are here to advise His Highness the prince, not His Majesty the king, you should direct your remarks to *him*.'

I looked at Amal, he held a silencing but reassuring

hand up to me. He was listening to their arguments.

'If we don't do it publicly,' the general continued, 'the ulama will say we've given in to the students and protestors.'

'They're already saying it,' the admiral added.

The police chief shook his head. 'It will just make things worse, there will be *more* demonstrations.'

'They've been demanding that the king be lenient,' one of the other men put in.

I nodded furiously, but no one was looking at me.

'They must be treated without mercy,' said the marshal, 'or we will see more jihadis, and I would rather face the students.'

'I can see the argument either way,' conceded the police chief.

'You can't behead people in the street!' I shouted over the discussion.

Daniel locked on me. 'They are terrorists, Mr Hollow, they killed two police officers. They cannot be given a slap on the wrist.'

'It's barbaric!'

A thin smile graced his lips. 'So that is what you think of us? Barbarians, just like all Arabs, yes?'

'That's not what I said.'

'You would prefer we take a more Western approach? We could let these men go back to their families, and then launch a drone strike on their house?'

A knowing titter rippled around the room.

'That too, is barbaric.' I spoke through clenched teeth. 'Government should exist to *prevent* murder, not franchise it.'

'You seem to be under a misconception. This discussion is not about whether we should execute these terrorists, but whether we should execute them in al-Abu Square. The law is the law. It cannot, and *should not*, be ignored.'

Everyone nodded.

'Public beheading in al-Abu Square, or firing squad in jail.'

I started again: 'Surely mercy—'

'That's enough Ben!' Amal barked.

I glared at him, but kept my trap shut.

Trying to conceal a satisfied smile, Daniel continued: 'The problem is as follows: if we hold to tradition and behead these men publicly the students will claim all our reforms have been for nothing and we will see more demonstrations. If we show leniency, and execute these men in prison, the ulama will claim we have capitulated and that will drive more into the arms of the terrorists.'

They all sat in silence for a moment, considering. Daniel, his stool on the dais, looked down on them all, giving them enough time to feel lost before continuing:

'Thus, I propose a third solution: we execute the

men by firing squad... in al-Abu Square. To the ulama say we have executed them publicly, to the students we have shown them leniency. Thoughts, gentlemen?'

The police chief nodded enthusiastically. 'That sounds like a fine solution. You've done it again, Daniel.'

'Very well,' said the general.

The rest just nodded, except Amal.

'Your Highness?' Daniel asked him. All eyes turned to him, including mine, pleading.

He nodded once. Daniel looked to the king, who nodded once.

I was furious. 'For the record,' I stated calmly, 'I think this is wrong.'

Daniel's eyes were as cold as marble. 'There is no record, Mr Hollow.'

'I'm sorry to put you in your place,' Amal told me that evening, looking out at the dying sun over my garden. 'But I could feel it in Daniel's voice: he had already decided. He had that solution up his sleeve from the beginning, the rest was just a show.'

'Why bother?'

'You have to sell the problem before the solution. And because making the decision into a group compromise strokes people's egos, and it makes them complicit if things go wrong. I've seen him do it before, been bamboozled by it myself. He suggests something outrageous, and you say you'll never agree to it, so he suggests a compromise, and that you agree to; after all, you're a reasonable guy; feeling that at the least you won some ground. Only when he's left do you get the distinct feeling that he got everything he wanted.'

He went back to staring for a few minutes. Then added, 'My father's rule is absolute, and whilst he's on the throne things will continue to be done Daniel's way.'

'Public executions?' A seismometer could have detected the tone in my voice.

'Criminals will continue to be executed in this country during my lifetime, and long after I'm dead. That is just a fact. If America still executes people, what hope do we have to put an end to it here?'

'My country stopped executing people fifty years ago.'

'Most of my country hasn't had electricity for fifty years. Some of it still doesn't.'

'Then add that to the list.'

'What list?' He turned towards me finally.

'The list of things you can do when you take the throne.'

He raised his eyebrows. 'That benevolent monarchy we argued about?'

'You have a chance to build your country anew. To

rake the soil and create an environment where democracy could flourish.'

He was silent for a long time. I watched fears and possibilities dance over his face like light and shade. When they settled, and the dying sun haloed him, he spoke:

'So, we'll electrify the outer settlements; we'll even give them broadband. We'll pave the streets. Build schools and hospitals. Enshrine equal rights in law. Give the people everything they don't know they need. And when we've done enough, when the wolves are already at the door, and enough people think they could run the country better than me, we'll start holding elections.'

Over the next three weeks we discussed far more mundane items at the weekly audiences, such as how to integrate the general's troops into the police force, and what duties they should perform. The answer was pairing them one to one, and only for perfunctory duties such as patrols and checkpoints. We discussed the level of irrigation required to support new farms on the outer reaches of the city, (too much). Fishing disputes with neighbouring countries, (perform some military exercises, remind them who has the bigger stick). Education programs, (great, but there are better places to invest money). Whether to allocate space outside the Albahr district to the growing number of Western and Asian firms wanting to set up regional offices, (simply redraw the boundaries and displace some of the migrants in neighbouring districts). Whether to accept a Chinese deal to build new infrastructure in exchange for a fifteen percent stake in ArgOil, (tempting, but too high a price). We discussed the imminent depletion of the oil fields, the potential discovery of new ones out at sea, and the investment and infrastructure that would be required to exploit them, (a gargantuan amount, but worth it). We discussed Israel (aggressive), we discussed Saudi Arabia (aggressive), we discussed America, Europe, even Brexit (uncertain), and many, many more things I knew nothing about. I contributed the odd detail-less probing question, just to remind people I was there.

The rest of the time I spent in meetings with Amal, mostly with American and European businessmen, looking for reassurances that their latest investments and endeavours would not come to nought. That the monarchy had their best interests at heart—No, rather that their interests were one and the same. I read everything I could, and it was never enough. But more and more I came to understand that Amal's current job, and perhaps his future job, was far more about managing people than details. Knowing who to listen to, and who to ignore. Who to praise, and who to admonish. It was simply about persuading people that whatever needed to be done would be good for them in the long run, and that they would not be left behind.

It was one month and one week to the day since my arrival when I found myself attending Mark Lowden's latest "empire party". It consisted of him and around thirty friends packed into what seemed like a small house, such had my mind been warped by the palaces I lived and worked in. One woman was dressed as Britannia, another as Margaret Thatcher, everyone else came as disconnected posh Brits, it was like university again. On the television a recorded football match played, muted, from the speakers came S Club 7. On a buffet table there were cheese and crackers with Branston pickle, papadums and mango chutney, and fruit scones with clotted cream and jam. The only British drink was Iron Brew.

'Where are you living?' was the first real question Mark asked me.

'In a little complex, a long way outside the city.'

'On the desert road?'

'Yes.'

'Wow! You're living in Raj Ranch.' He turned to the others: 'Hey, guys! Ben is living in Raj Ranch.'

'Cool!' came one of the replies. The others did not care.

'What's Raj Ranch?' I asked.

'Oh, sorry, we call it that because of the Indian Raj, you know. It was built for the American families who came here to work as part of Argamoil. Back when they ran the company. Part of that post-war optimism that lasted all of half a decade.'

'You seem to know everything about this place.'

'It pays for the company to be well-informed. People like me probably aren't supposed to know, but knowledge is like jelly: the tighter you try to keep hold of it, the more it slips through your fingers.'

I smiled at the image of jelly squirting out Daniel's grip. I lowered my voice just enough: 'How much do know about the men captured in the Albahr district?'

'The ones they executed?'

I nodded. 'I didn't see anything in the paper until the execution was arranged.'

He scoffed, 'Well, you wouldn't, would you? They're not allowed to mention the rebels.'

I wondered for a moment how much ignorance I should reveal to this smiling blonde gentleman. This moment of indecision was enough:

'How much do you know about them?' he asked.

All I did was look at him. He grabbed me by the arm and led me into his study, quietly shutting the door behind us.

'I guess they've got a pretty good stranglehold on your information flow. So...' he thought about where to begin, 'how much do I have to tell you? The rebels are based in the smaller communities that still dot the land outside the city. Not the ones on the coast, because they're protected by the navy, and not where you are, as that's too close to the army barracks. I mean, no one really knows where they are, that's why they still exist.'

'What do they want?'

'They believe that the government is corrupt, even by Arab standards, and that the monarchy must be overthrown, and a new democratic government established. Their leader is a man called Bahadur, sometimes people call him "the Turk".'

'He's not from Argolis then?'

'I don't know. No one knows anything about him.'

'Then why do they call him the Turk?'

'I don't know. Maybe they're afraid to say his name. People are forbidden from mentioning him, or the rebels.'

'It's a crime?'

He scoffed again. 'It's not like it's on the statute book, it's just something everyone knows not to do.'

'So you're saying these men weren't terrorists?'

He made an uncertain face. 'It's not that simple. They're not jihadis, but they did enter the Albahr district with guns, they did kill two police officers.'

'So they *are* terrorists?'

He sighed. 'Well, not according to the BBC. The

government are as much a target for real terrorists, Islamic fundamentalists, as all governments in the Middle East.'

'Ok. And they're connected with the students, right?'

'No. Not exactly. The university is a radical place, like all universities, but the students who protest for democracy do it peacefully. Although some of them do go on to join the rebels. And the government can't close the university because that's where most the country's doctors and teachers come from.'

'So why did the rebels kill police officers?'

'They were obviously there to do more. The rebels are fighting a war, they're a resistance, trying to overthrow a tyrannical government, in their eyes. Whereas you know what al-Nusra and IS want: they want a caliphate, governed by a backwards interpretation of Islam that only survived the eighteenth century because it was useful to the Saudis.'

'So why did the police say these men were terrorists?'

'Because that's what the government do. From their side, all these groups want to overthrow them; they want to string Daniel al-Hadi and his like up from the lamp posts. The king, they'd probably have the good decency just to shoot. So when the students protest, the government say they're rebels; and when the rebels stage an attack, they scream terrorists.'

I tried desperately to catch the questions that had

spent three weeks tearing round my head. 'And the "ulama", who are they?'

'They're the religious leaders. They're Islamic fundamentalists too, but they won't kill people over it. The government is caught between the students and the rebels on one side, and the ulama and IS on the other. They have to keep the scales balanced. That's Daniel al-Hadi's wizardry.'

'How does he do it?'

'The king is seen as very traditional, so he has to make frequent little reforms to please the students. Your man is seen as a liberal, so he'll have to be pretty tough to please the ulama.'

'But how can the king be seen as traditional if he keeps making reforms? How can the prince be seen as liberal if he keeps capitulating to the ulama?'

'Because of what he says, who he's seen with, how old he is.'

'So they say one thing, and do another. And people are satisfied with that?'

'Welcome to politics.'

More questions were born and scampered off into the dark. I left them to it, I was occupied with other thoughts.

He read my mind: 'You made the right decision.' He even put a hand on my shoulder. 'Look at where *our* country is at the moment. It's being pulled back into the past, ripped apart, and the pieces that are left will fall into the hands of fascists and Marxists. This country is the future.'

6

Kings of Kings

IT WAS THREE O'CLOCK in the morning when I woke to the sound of a woman wailing. I could hear it coming from the balcony, ten metres from the end of my bed, the doors to which I always left open. I sat up, watching the moonlit voiles flutter in breeze. After a minute of hushed breathing, I slid out from the sheets and tiptoed across the room. Under the stars, the balcony was empty. The sound was coming from below. I leant over to see the woman weeping in the arms of Abderrazzaq, my butler. The sounds of televisions and radios drifted on the pregnant air. There was a buzz about, the servants knew something.

I threw on a dressing gown and marched through the silent house. The five starlit rooms I passed through seemed like cold planets as I made my way down two sets of stairs and into the staff wing. Abderrazzaq was now in his office, with two of the maids, all staring at a small television screen showing tomorrow's weather. The maids jumped out of their skin when they saw me.

'Sir?' Abderrazzaq said with a touch of concern.

'What's going on?'

He gave a look to the maids but they had already vanished. His domed, bald scalp was wet with perspiration. 'It's just a rumour, sir. From my cousin... he...' He looked down, trying to find the right words.

'What is it?'

'He has heard... that the king has died.'

This news did not land as heavily as you might think. I had stopped believing anything I was told. 'Who is your cousin?'

'He works in the household of General Othman, but his son is a driver for the king's doctor.'

'Do you have a telephone number for him?'

'The switchboard is engaged, sir. I have tried, but no calls can get in or out.'

Something was up. 'Wake Munir, if he's not up already, I need to get to the palace. Ten minutes.'

He nodded and hurried off. I jogged back to my rooms, threw on clothes, and was down outside the front in twelve minutes.

Munir was leaning on the bonnet, smoking a cigarette, half his shirt buttons misaligned. He spat the cigarette a mile when he saw me and darted behind the wheel.

'Is it true, sir?' he asked when we had cleared the compound and made it onto the empty arrow of tarmac towards the city.

'I don't know,' I replied gently, 'I don't know.'

He went to turn on the radio.

'Leave it off,' I told him, preferring to stare in silence at the undulating waves of silver sand.

Twenty minutes later we had slipped through the silent city and skidded to a stop outside the palace. I jumped out and told Munir to wait where he could.

In the main entrance hall various security men were loitering like left luggage. As I went to enter the residence a palace guard stepped in my way:

'Sorry, sir.'

Before I had a chance to protest I heard 'Let him in,' barked from behind my ear and General Othman stormed past the man.

I had to skip to keep up with him. 'What's happened?'

'You probably know more than I do.'

He ascended quickly up two flights of stairs, past more guards, down a corridor, then pushed through double doors into an antechamber. Daniel al-Hadi leapt out of a plush red chair, looking as immaculate, and irritated by my presence, as ever.

'What's going on?' the general barked.

Daniel spoke in a whisper. 'The family are in with him now. He won't last the night.'

We stood in silence for a moment, all of us equalled by the significance of the situation.

Daniel returned to his chair, the general took another, and I a third, there were at least ten more empty. I played with my fingernails, Daniel stared into an abyss, and the general seemed to have switched his brain off entirely.

Twenty minutes of silence was interrupted by the night call to prayer. In Argolis that meant it was two hours before dawn.

The sound seemed to untether me from reality, and I felt myself being pulled downwards towards the blackness of sleep. Neither Daniel nor the general got up to pray, both looked halfway to a new dimension. Then, just as the mu'addhin had finished and silence returned, the chief of police burst through the doors, huffing and puffing, and jolted us all out of our trance. He headed straight for the nearest chair and began mopping his sweaty brow.

When he had regained his breath he asked, 'How is he?'

'Not well. This is it,' replied Daniel.

'No chance it's a false alarm?'

'Not this time.'

The chief let out a long low whistle. He shook his

head, stopped, started shaking it again. He kept repeating this for five minutes. Eventually, he spoke: 'I remember my father telling me about the day al-Abu died.'

'I remember it,' Daniel mused, 'I was twelve years old. Most people didn't own a television, or even a radio, it was shouted from the rooftops, and anyone who didn't hear read it in tomorrow's newspaper.' He sighed. 'I didn't understand: how could the king die?'

'My father told me it was the only time he ever cried.'

'I fear the response this time will be somewhat more nuanced.'

The chief took a cigarette from his breast pocket and began rolling it around in his fingers, when he noticed what he was doing he quickly put it back away. 'How do we report it?' he asked.

'We certainly don't report that the king is dying. And we don't report that he has died without a statement from the prince.'

General Othman pitched in: 'If we stay silent too long people will come up with their own ideas.'

'There are rumours he's dead already,' I added.

Daniel shot me an accusatory look, but it quickly evolved into concern. 'If we report that he is dying there will be panic. If we report his death without a strong and unifying statement from the new king, everyone desperate to seize control will see this as their moment. This is the most dangerous night of our lives.'

'W-what do we do?' the chief asked on the edge of panic.

'You need to get your men out on the streets, quietly. The general's men too.'

'I've already sent word to wake every man we have,' the general reassured him.

'What did you tell them?' the chief asked.

'They're soldiers, I don't have to tell them anything.'

'My men are police officers, what do I tell *them*?'

'Tell them they'll be timed,' Daniel offered, 'they'll assume it's a drill.'

'Timed... right.'

The chief left the room, groping for his phone.

'When the people see police and soldiers in the street, will that make them feel more or less alarmed?' I asked.

'More alarmed if there is nothing from us to tell them what is going on. But nonetheless, the first voice they hear must be the prince's. And that will not happen whilst he is in that room.'

We all looked towards the dark wooden doors, meshed with gold filigree, so tall they loomed over us.

He wandered to the solitary window, opening it an inch. 'We will have to hope everyone sleeps well tonight.' Next he opened the doors behind us and leant out to one of the palace guards. 'What is the weather like this evening?'

'Cold, sir,' came the voice. 'There's a sea mist coming in.'

'Thank you.' He shut the doors again. 'Cold and misty, that will do us some favours should the king—' he stopped himself, 'should we be waiting a while longer.'

We took our seats again. An hour passed, most of which I slept. I dreamt I was wandering in a forest, my pace picking up against my wishes until I was hurtling in all directions at once, not knowing which one I wanted. I was roused by the distant echoing sound of a twig snapping. Followed by two or three more.

'What was that?' Daniel blurted with a voice also roused from sleep.

The general marched to the small window, the wind on his moustache. 'Gunfire.'

The three of us stood in silence, listening desperately, waiting for it to flare up in earnest. We held our breath as though we might set off an avalanche.

What seemed like an age later, but must only have been a couple of minutes, the police chief burst through the doors like they were the finish line of a marathon.

'What the hell is going on?' Daniel demanded.

'Two stupid punks...' he gasped between breaths, his face swollen and red as he bent over, leaning on his knees, '...shooting a dog.'

'Why were these "punks" armed?'

The chief looked up with trepidation.

'Please don't tell me the answer is they're police officers.'

'They're only young, fresh. They've already been taken off the streets. I'll deal with them.'

'Do, or I will.'

Real fear crossed the chief's face. 'I'll deal with them.'

'It'll be getting light soon,' the general mused from the window.

'We need to say something.' The chief's voice might have come from another room.

'We can't do anything without the prince!' Daniel snapped.

'What if...' the chief started, 'what if the prince were to record his message early, so it could be played the moment the king... I mean, at the earliest possible time?'

Daniel considered it for a moment, sucking his teeth. 'I suppose if the prince were to prepare his remarks in advance it would allow us to console the public at the most opportune moment. But that won't happen until he leaves that room.'

'Someone needs to go in there,' the general mused further.

All three turned to look at me.

I balked. 'I think the case would be better made by you—' I blurted at Daniel, but he cut me off:

'Maybe, but I am more concerned for the prince's wellbeing,' he purred, 'it would be best, given the degree of tact required, for him to hear it from a friend.'

I hesitated.

'You would be doing him a great service.'

The chief nodded, mumbling 'Yes, yes, great service.'

I could feel the pressure of all six eyeballs, all waiting to find out what I was bringing to this party, if anything.

If I was going to do it, I had to own it. I nodded firmly, calmly, and moved confidently to open the door. As I approached the handle it swung inwards, and there they stood, shuffling out. Amal, his mother, sister, two young children (a boy and a girl) whom I presumed were his sister's, and an old man I supposed was the doctor. Amal's and his mother's eyes were red, their faces raw. Beyond their shoulders the king lay tucked up in a four-poster bed, now forever asleep.

The same simple shroud. The same stony cemetery. I prepared myself for the same disrespectful wake, but instead of a rowdy party it was a more age-appropriate state banquet.

One long table snaked its way around the main hall, covered with crisp white linen and decked with ornate gilded plates, glasses, and oil lamps; food was served and removed by silent staff. I was placed in a sea of unfamiliar faces, who largely ignored me, expect a kind old man on my right who tried though only knowing four words of English to engage me in conversation. Although I smiled and tried hard, he had abandoned the attempt by the second course.

My attention was captivated by another old man, sitting just a few places down the table from me, on the other side, close enough to observe, but too far to speak or even listen to. He was the only other non-Arab, with thinning white hair and a thick white beard, and something imperceptible told me he was English. He nodded along earnestly, occasionally enthusiastically, to what his neighbour was telling him. He wore a beige suit with elbow patches, checked white shirt, and faded red tie. They all looked as though he had been wearing them for thirty years.

After the meal I managed to move myself into a conversation with him, now sitting on a chair in the main courtyard under a star strewn sky. His name was Martin, he was retired and lived in a small country cottage off the South Downs. He had known the king, become good friends as younger men when he worked for Argamoil, living in the very complex I now haunted; but when he moved back to England to marry they drifted apart. He had not seen the king for thirty years, not been to Argolis for fifty. I was fascinated.

'What was he like back then?'

'In the beginning? Hot-headed. We both were.' He gave an embarrassed and apologetic smile. 'This country was the same age you are now. Did you know both Abdullah and I were born the same year this country was? His father may have founded it, but it lived and breathed in Abdullah.'

'How did he feel about his father?'

'He was proud of him, he had done something no one in the history of his people had ever done: unified the tribes, and driven off us British. But Abdullah believed passionately that progress needed to continue, that his father was complacent with what he had achieved. He wanted to transform this country...'

I gave a meek smile.

'And he did!' He gestured to the top of a skyscraper that twinkled like a torch through the evening haze. 'When I last saw this place there was not a single paved road. Hardly any running water. What little electricity there was ran off petrol generators. He's brought companies to the city, a university, hospitals, schools. He's driven the Americans out of Argamoil, given the oil back to the people, like he always said he would. An Arab city, self-reliant, that others flock to for work. That new Constantinople we always dreamed of. I'm proud of him.' He gave me a sympathetic smile. 'And I'm sure his son will continue that transformation.' He sighed. 'I wish I could see this place in another fifty years.'

'Why did you never come back?'

The corners of his mouth turned up, but his eyes were melancholy. 'There's an age when you have to stop living in your dream.'

I let that hang in the air, I had no desire to argue dreams with a pessimist. I made small talk: 'Did your wife travel with you here?'

His face was impassive. 'She left me years ago.'

I did my best to ignore the thud as that hit the table. 'Are you going to stay awhile,' I offered instead, 'explore the country he built?'

'I don't think so. If I'm not willing to live in my own dream, I certainly can't live in someone else's.'

Amal had no formal coronation. It was not how things were done. But once his father was buried, it was considered appropriate to have a small celebration. The palace was stocked and dressed much as it had been for his brother's wake, but where the guests then had been Iman's friends and hangers-on, the guests at this banquet were lucky ticket holders: people the family and Amal's circle wanted there, and many, many more who had paid for their ticket. Not that the process was so openly vulgar, the crowd that pushed and fought for what little food there seemed to be were those who knew someone, or knew someone who knew someone, or knew someone who knew someone who could bribe someone. It was the only thing that accounted for the sheer number of them: the gig had been considerably oversold. Everything below the tops of columns and the ceiling with its pyramidal lights was hidden by the drowning masses.

I bumped and shoved my way through the writhing sea of suit vents, hoping to find Amal, but where before I had been invisible, now I was positively magnetic. Backs became shirts and ties, people were drawn towards me; businessmen, dignitaries, everyone thought I had the king's ear and wanted me to pour something in it. I felt like bait in a shark tank.

'Ah, it's Mr Hollow, isn't it?' they would shout over the deafening racket of too many people in a hard-walled room, as though they would know my name without finding out deliberately.

This time it was a tall and narrow old Englishman whose domed scalp stubbornly held on to a few hairs. He wore a black suit and faded college tie. Behind him, nodding sheepishly, stood Mark Lowden.

'My name is Fettiplace, Edward Fettiplace, I run the Persian Gulf operations of Geosis, based here in Argolis.' He held out a hand.

I shook it. 'Nice to meet you, Mr Fettiplace.'

He gave my hand a tight squeeze, either deliberately to convince me he was not as old as he looked, or as an involuntary reaction to having to schmooze someone so young. 'We've done Argamoil plenty of favours over the years.' His best shout failed to extinguish his disdain.

His condescension irritated me. 'It's ArgOil now, Mr Fettiplace, not Argamoil. And no doubt you've reaped a lot of business in return for your favours.'

He swallowed. 'Yes, well, I just hope it won't be forgotten by the new king.'

'Are you still the best at what you do?'

'Of course.'

'Then you have nothing to worry about.'

He mumbled, 'Glad to hear it,' and shuffled away. Mark Lowden was grinning as he followed.

I stood still for five seconds too long.

'Mr Hollow, I believe,' a short fat brown man announced theatrically.

I was not listening. I had spotted across the shoals of heads my mysterious friend from the Loch Ness party.

'Excuse me,' I told the man to his disappointment, and tried to swim against the current towards my friend. He was watching and raised a glass of champagne to me with a devilish smile. He began to pivot out of sight like a reflection on the surface and I swam harder to keep him in view, bumping straight into a sixty-something silver-haired man in a smart suit. He looked like a movie star. I recognised him, but from where?

'Mr Hollow, I presume.' Out came his hand.

I shook it, it was very soft. A man stood at his left arm, watching me. He had the coiled earpiece of a security man.

'Ben, my Institute for Middle East Peace would be very interested in setting up a meeting with the king. Perhaps that's something you could arrange?'

That voice. That smile. The floor crumbled under my feet; this was a man whose poster I had had on my bedroom wall. The most successful Prime Minister in the history of my party. The very man I aspired to be.

I managed to stumble over two words: 'Of course!'

'Brill. I'm a great admirer of his, I think he's going to do incredible things.'

I just nodded stupidly, trying to shake some life into my tongue. How he interpreted my lack of response I'm not sure, but he looked mildly disappointed, which was not my intent.

'Anyway,' he continued, 'sorry we can't chat, I have a flight to Jordan leaving in ninety minutes.' He grinned, 'Bloody speaking engagements.'

He walked past me, patting me on the shoulder as he went. The security man gave me the raised eyebrows of being impressed.

It was then I realised I was not bait in the shark tank.

I was the big fish that the little cleaner fish come to nibble off.

I looked across the bobbing heads to see Amal's glowing under a golden light. He was surrounded by men all desperate just to be looked at by him. When he saw me over them, a broad smile cracked across his face, and he winked. I knew then that we were going to do incredible things.

Part III

And on the pedestal, these words appear:
My name is Ozymandias, King of Kings;
Look on my Works, ye Mighty, and despair!

Ozymandias, Percy Bysshe Shelley

7

The Hand That Mocked Them

THE ROOM SHOOK; rumbling, creaking, tinkling; I felt the shuddering in my chest. A sound like thunder broke through the walls. I launched out of bed, catching my foot on the sheet and falling onto all fours. The marble floor vibrated under my hands. Then it stopped, and the tinkling slowly died.

I ran to the balcony, from there I could hear others rushing and shouting, but could not see anything helpful. I looked back towards my room, and only then could I see an orange glow in the sky. I ran into the corridor, and up to a window that looked out over the front of the house. Others were outside. I could see towards the main gate of the complex, and beyond the desert road, across the sand where the sky glowed orange and the sun seemed to peek above the horizon. At two o'clock in the morning.

When I reached the ground floor I bumped into Abderrazzaq.

'What's going on, sir? Is it the Americans? Are they invading?'

'It's not the Americans,' I chided him.

'What is it then?'

I avoided answering. 'Make sure everyone is accounted for, get them gathered in the kitchen. Keep them calm. When you've done that, get me the palace on the phone.'

I stepped out the front, towards the crowd that had run from their houses, the cord of my dressing gown trailing behind. When they spotted me they went silent; since the coronation, word had got round of who I was. They stared at me with anxious and expectant white faces. I did not know who any of them were, just birds in gilded cages.

'What's in that direction?' I asked.

There was silence for a few moments until a voice at the back cleared his throat and said: 'The oil fields.'

I nodded, and headed back to the house. Abderrazzaq was in a tizzy in the hallway.

'Is it a coup!?'

'Have you got through to the palace yet?' I barked.

'No, sir, it's the same as before: the phone lines are busy.'

I fiddled with my dressing gown cord for thirty seconds. 'Ok, get Munir to bring the car round.'

Nine minutes later I was dressed and the car was out front, Munir staring at the horizon like all the others. He shot me a look of fear as we jumped in.

We crawled slowly to the gate, through the parting clumps of people. At the gate a man carrying an assault rifle stepped from the guardhouse and waved his hand at the car. The gate stayed shut. The man knocked on Munir's window and spoke to him in Arabic.

'He says we cannot leave,' Munir told me.

'Tell him who I am.'

He did. 'He says he knows, sir, but it's his job to keep you safe. The compound is locked down until the police or the army give the all clear.'

I sighed. 'Fine, take us back.'

We crawled back through the crowd, who now looked even more confused. When we pulled up outside my house a large American who had jogged alongside the car poked a pudgy finger at me and shouted:

'You work for the king, right? What's going on?'

Others gathered towards me, drawn by the noise.

'I don't know,' I told him honestly.

'Can't you find out!?'

'The phones are busy.'

'I've got a satphone.' He pushed it at me.

'That won't make any difference if the call is trying

to connect to a landline the other end.'

'Then what are we supposed to do!?'

'Keep calm and watch the news.'

'Oh yeah, great. They're the *last* to know.'

'The World Service then,' I barked.

As he started to leave I had a brainwave. 'Give me the satellite phone.'

He was suddenly less keen to hand it to me.

'I'll let you know what I find out,' I assured him.

He placed it in my palm like a brick.

'Now get everyone back inside. Whatever happens, it won't help having everyone blocking the gate.'

He nodded reluctantly and jogged off into the crowd.

I marched back inside, passing no one, up to my office, and flipped open my laptop. Few people in Argolis had mobile phones, and as a result there was a chance the network would still have capacity. I had given up my mobile since the only masts were in the city, miles away. And I did not have a mobile number for Amal, nor anyone in his circle, but I could get the number of someone who might know what was going on.

I searched for Mark Lowden's most recent email, his number was in the signature. It rang.

'Hello?' he answered cautiously.

'Mark, it's Ben. Sorry to call you so late.'

He scoffed. 'That's all right, I think everyone's

awake.'

'What's happened?'

'You must know more than me.' He sounded groggy.

'I don't know a thing.'

There was a pause. 'Where are you calling from?'

'Home.'

'How did you get through?'

'On a satellite phone, but that's not important. What's going on?'

'I don't know; I'll try to find out. Give me a few minutes and I'll call you back, ok?'

'Yes, fine.'

'Are you heading to the palace?'

'I can't, this place is locked down.'

'Ok, ok...' he sounded preoccupied, 'I'll call you back.' He hung up.

I sat in my office chair for forty minutes, I did not want to leave the room without more information than when I entered it. Finally, the phone rang and I snapped it up.

'Mark!?'

'Yes, sorry it took so long. Things are a bit manic here.'

'What's happened?'

'There's been some kind of explosion at the oil fields. IS are claiming responsibility for it, but there's no confirmation yet.'

'Was it a bomb then?'

'We don't know, but it does seem likely: oil tends to burn, not explode. It's burning *now* of course; half the fields are on fire.' There was another pause, and a sigh. 'Ben, we've got people out there, we need to know what the military are planning to do. If they're sending in the emergency services we can leave it to them, but if they're not sending them we'll have to send our own people. But we can't send in a rescue mission if they're going to get caught in crossfire between the army and IS.'

I scratched my head, I did not know what to do.

'Ben, they're British citizens, trapped in a burning oil field, with terrorists trying to kill them; is there no one you can call?'

I had a think.

He did not like the silence: 'We need to know what the military are planning.'

'I'll see what I can do.'

'Thank you, Ben. Please hurry.'

I hung up.

I tapped on the desk for a minute, thinking my way out of the complex, projecting all the way to the palace. When I opened my eyes I was still in my office, still clutching the satellite phone.

I went downstairs, searching the servants' quarters for Abderrazzaq. Eventually I found him in the larder, obsessively turning tins and packets so that they faced forwards.

'Abderrazzaq?'

'Sir!?' He jumped. 'Is everything ok?'

'Your cousin is a driver for General Othman, correct?

'No, sir, he's just a caretaker in the house. His son is a driver for the king's doctor—I mean, the old king's doctor.'

'Right, yes, that was it. Does your cousin have a mobile phone?'

He shook his head as though the idea was ridiculous. 'Damn.'

'His son does, sir. So that he can be called to drive the doctor at any time.'

My slim chance had got slimmer, but it was still there. 'Can you call him—do you have his number?'

'Of course, sir.'

I held out the satellite phone. 'I need you to call him, and get him to drive over to the palace. If anyone tries to stop him, tell him to get me on the phone.'

The phone conversation was loud and fast, Abderrazzaq's panic difficult to read.

It was only fifteen minutes before I got my first call. A brusque voice spoke in Arabic.

'Who is this?' I barked.

The man explained, in very terse English, that he was the head of palace security, and that a man claiming to be acting on my orders was blocking the main gate, insisting that he must be allowed to enter the palace. They were on high alert for terrorist attacks, and a strange man without identification had driven an empty chauffeured car to the palace gates and insisted on being let in. His men were aiming machine guns at the car as we spoke.

I summoned an authority into my voice that I had never achieved before: 'My name is Benedict Hollow. You know who I am. The man is indeed following my orders. Either let him in, or deliver my message to the king yourself.'

There was a pause of about ten seconds. 'What is the message?'

'To call me on this number immediately.'

'I will deliver the message.'

'Very well, I will telephone you in ten minutes if I have not received a call. I have your name.'

He hung up.

Six minutes later the phone rang again.

'Mr Hollow,' the voice purred.

'Where is he, Daniel?'

'I'm afraid the king is in the middle of an important military briefing and cannot be disturbed.'

'I need to speak to him.'

'And I will make sure to encourage him to call you, once the current situation has been resolved.'

'No, Daniel, you will take whatever phone you are holding right now and you will put it to his ear.'

'That would involve quite a lot of reconstruction to the palace, and would probably not suit your needs in terms of the timescale required.'

'In the nicest possible terms, Daniel, I don't have time for your bullshit.'

There was a soft exhaling of breath on the other end of the line. Then his voice was low, without play: 'Were you here in person, Mr Hollow, I would have no problem with escorting you into the briefing room to offer your—no doubt—*expert* military advice. But I cannot begin to explain to you the security risks involved with the king calling you on an unknown, unsecure phone, in the middle of a military crisis.'

'Isn't that up to the king to decide?'

'He has bigger decisions to make right now. Goodbye.'

'No—' I cried, but it was too late, he had hung up.

I tapped my index finger on the desk at an energetic tempo. My leg was shaking. I was not going to let Daniel al-Hadi get his way again.

I telephoned the guard.

'I delivered your message, sir,' he said with confusion.

'I know, I need you to deliver one more. This time to General Othman, directly, no one but him, you understand?'

'Yes, sir. But the general is not here yet.'

I could curse Daniel: the king cloistered in an important military briefing and yet the head of the army is not even there.

'Fine. Call me the second he—'

'His car is arriving now, sir.'

'Put him on the phone!'

I heard fumbling and heated exchanges for around a minute, the general's husky voice came on the line.

'Ben?'

'Yes, general. What is going on, what's happening?'

'I don't have time to brief you, Ben, aren't you coming to the palace?'

'I can't, the complex is locked down.'

He grumbled. 'I'll send my car for you.'

'Thank you, general, but first I need to know what you're planning to do. There are people trapped on the oil fields, they need ambulances, are you sending in the emergency services?'

'Can't send the emergency services into a warzone, Ben, but there'll be army ambulances with our troops. You tell anyone who's thinking of sending people in there to keep the hell out. They'll only get themselves killed, and we won't be held responsible for anyone else's stupidity. You understand?'

'Yes, general. Thank you for sending the car, tell him to hurry.'

He grumbled again, then he hung up.

I called Mark, told him what he had told me.

'Thank you, Ben. I guess we'll have to hold tight and hope for the best. Thank you, again. I'll let you rest.'

I was just dressed and caffeinated by the time the general's car arrived. The guards recognised it immediately and let it in; the tinted windows preventing them from knowing it was empty. I hopped in before they could inspect it and off I sped, thrown back into my seat.

'I'm sorry, sir,' the driver said into the rear-view mirror, 'but the general said to get you there as quickly as possible.'

By the time I made it to the palace the decision had already been made. The general had got his way: solders were sent in, with army ambulances in support. When they made it to the epicentre they found the perpetrators were already dead, caught in the explosion. Whether this was deliberate could not be established. Three security guards had been killed as the bombers infiltrated the complex, but no one else. The worst had been avoided, I thought.

In the morning the fire was still raging. It would burn for another three days, the smoke turning the sky yellower than the sand, the sun blood red, the world dim.

'It will take six months, at the minimum, to repair

the oil fields and restore them back to full operation. It will be three months before they produce anything at all,' Daniel explained at the next audience. Under Amal's reign he had been relegated to the semi-circle, and I was on dais.

'What effect is that going to have on the public finances?' I asked him.

Daniel swallowed. 'Crude oil represents ninety-two percent of government revenues, and seventy percent of GDP. Even taking into account our financial reserves, we are looking at a catastrophic hole in the public purse.'

'You will just have to borrow more,' I replied.

'We will already have to borrow considerable amounts to fund the repairs; we will be unable to borrow much more without devaluing our bonds, and when that happens creditors will start cashing them in for cash we do not have.'

'Then print more money.'

'That would make the already considerable risk of hyperinflation more likely, lead to a devaluation of our currency; and if our currency is worth less the repairs will cost more.'

'Then what do you suggest?' I sighed.

'Since there is a reduction in our incomings, we must meet it with a reduction in our outgoings.'

'How exactly?'

'A temporary pay-reduction for all government

workers. Obviously, we cannot reduce it by ninety-two percent, but by a considerable amount: fifty percent. The remainder can be covered by new borrowing.'

'My men will understand,' said the general.

The police chief, admiral, and marshal squirmed in their seats.

'No, that's absurd,' I told Daniel, 'just increase business taxes.'

'No,' he snapped.

'The businesses in the Albahr district profit from the oil production, it is only fair they pay for its repair.'

'Those businesses will simply leave the country, Mr Hollow, and then we will be in a worse situation.'

'Then tax the small businesses; the shops, the street-sellers.'

'The immigrants? Perhaps we could beg in the street? It would raise about as much.'

A couple of the others sniggered.

I huffed. Then I tried to hammer my point into his impenetrable skull: 'Almost every Argolisian citizen works for the government, correct?'

'Yes,' he condescended.

'How are they going to feel as they get poorer and the immigrants they see all around them are left un-touched?'

'They are immigrants, as you say: they come from Malaysia, Indonesia, India, Africa; the dregs of the world. Rats, they will leave this country on rafts the second it is not worth their while. But the citizens of this country will not desert, it is their country, and they will have to pay to put it back on its feet!' It was the first time I had heard him flustered. He calmed. 'But maybe you're right: if they leave, the citizens of this country will have to run their own shops. It might even help diversify the economy.'

'You're both right,' Amal declared. He stole everyone's attention, holding it in silence for at least half a minute before he announced his decision:

'Gentlemen, we need more money. We have to cover the gap in our finances. We can't borrow it, we can't print it, we can't tax businesses, we can't tax immigrants, not without threatening further damage. Yet we must contain the economic shock. Shutting down oil production has damaged our economy, we cannot let it destroy it.' He brought a ringed fist up to his mouth. 'I will not cut pay, but I *will* tax it: a fifty percent Repair Tax for all government employees. That includes you, gentlemen. And I will find a way to make a contribution from the royal household. I will make the speech this afternoon.'

✦

The royal family owned several London properties through a shell company in the British Virgin Islands; Amal began selling them immediately. They would raise seventy million pounds by the end of the month, mostly from Russian and Chinese buyers. He gave his speech live from the radio station:

'...we have been attacked by those who twist our religion into a weapon of hate against true Muslims. They have knocked us down, but together we will get back up stronger. Stronger because of the sacrifices we must make. My grandfather built this country, liberated us from imperialist oppression. My father fortified that promise, liberating us from the oppression of poverty. I, his son, will liberate us from the hatred that threatens to oppress us now. And together, we will make Argolis great again.'

8

Those Passions Red

DANCING DUST FLICKERED in the air above my head, travelling a long ray of sunlight that had sneaked in through the top of the shutters. I stretched my arms and legs out in a star shape, feeling nothing but sheets and mattress. I was wonderfully content. But then the light struck me again; what was it doing coming through that gap at this time? I reached over for my watch. It was eleven in the morning. I was normally woken with breakfast at eight o'clock. And there was an audience today!

I jumped out of bed, up to the open balcony windows and opened the shutters. The almost-midday sun beat down on me, the world was silent except for the gentle *phut-phut* of the sprinklers. I stepped back inside and threw on my dressing gown. I wandered down through empty rooms to the kitchen. Abderrazzaq was bent over the stove, attempting to fry an egg.

'What's going on?' I asked.

'Sir?' he said with confusion, turning to face me. Then he positively screamed.

I jumped out of my skin.

He apologised: 'Sir, sir, I am so sorry! Please, forgive me, I forgot of course that you would not be woken because there was no breakfast to deliver.'

'Why is there no breakfast?'

'I'm afraid, sir, there was no one to cook it.'

'Where's Omar?'

'He left, sir. He went to work in a restaurant in the city. He left without notice or I would have had someone to replace him.'

'He just up and left overnight?'

'No, sir, he left a week ago.'

'Then who's been cooking my meals for the last week?'

'My nephew, sir. He wants to study in Paris. He's very keen.'

'Well, he's better than no one, you had better get him on the payroll. Did Omar say why he suddenly wanted to leave?'

'Yes, sir, you see, working here, he's on the government payroll, and... he is subject to the new tax. He said,' his eyes looked down with embarrassment, 'he could earn more selling falafel on the street, sir. I am very ashamed, sir. I am in charge of running the house-hold. I will understand if you fire me.'

'Then I'll have no one. Don't be silly, just remember to wake me.'

'Is it true, sir, that the army do not have to pay the tax? The soldiers, I mean.'

'Of course not. Your egg is burning.'

'Thank you, sir.' He took the pan off the hob.

'Is Munir still with us?'

'Yes, sir.'

'Tell him to bring the car round in twenty minutes, but eat your egg first.'

'Thank you, sir.'

The city seemed empty as Munir drove me towards the palace. Lone children wandered normally busy streets. A dog tried to sleep in the middle of a four-lane high-way, barking at anything that passed. Even the front of the palace was empty of its usual string of black Mer-cedes.

As I jogged up the red-carpeted steps I passed Gen-eral Othman sauntering the other way.

'Have I missed it?'

'Missed what?' he asked as he kept moving.

I chased after him, grabbing his elbow and lowering my voice: 'General, is it true soldiers don't have to pay the tax?'

He chuckled to himself. 'I've heard my men ask the same about policemen.'

He started moving again. I turned back up the steps, into the main entrance hall, then down to the audience room, wrenching open the door to find it empty. The lights were off.

I moved into the empty corridors, passing only guards until I rounded a corner and saw Daniel in front of me, clutching some papers with a smile on his face, and leaning in to speak with Rania.

'Thank you,' he told her, 'you are as wise as you are beautiful, your highness.'

I stepped back, out of sight. Footsteps approached and Daniel came round the corner, stopping suddenly upon seeing me. His shock registered as a slow blink.

'Mr Hollow. Overslept, did we?'

I refused to rise to that. 'Pumping Rania, I see?'

'Excuse me!?' For a split-second he looked terrified.

'"You are as wise as you are beautiful, your highness," come on, what is it you want out of her?'

'I happen to admire the princess.'

I scoffed.

He looked offended.

I could not believe it: 'My god, you're telling the truth, aren't you? No wonder I couldn't tell. You don't want to get anything out of her. Quite the opposite, in fact.'

He looked like he might bite off his own tongue. For the first time, he seemed lost for words.

'What happened to the audience?' I asked.

'The king had to leave suddenly.'

'Where?'

'An emergency conference in Doha.'

'Doha? Why wasn't I told.'

'I believe the king instructed his people to call you but there was no answer at your house. Having problems, are we?'

I sighed. 'Fuck off.'

He blenched. I probably should not have said it, but tiredness and hunger had got the better of me. I marched off and out of the palace, back to the car.

Munir drove me back through the same empty streets until we stopped at the only set of traffic lights. Out of my window, down a narrow pedestrian street that led off our side of the road, I could see a market; and at the end of it a man at a stall selling something edible with a smile. Steam was rising from whatever it was and people were taking huge bites of it once they gratefully received the napkin-wrapped parcel. He was using tongs to turn them on a hot plate. I slid down a window just an inch. On a breeze of hot air the smell of cooking reached me. It was something savoury, I swore I could hear the sizzling.

The lights went green; Munir began to ease the accelerator pedal down, the revs increased.

'Wait.'

The sound of the engine died back down. 'Sir?'

'Pull over, I'm going to get something to eat.'

'Sir?'

'Come on, I'm starving, pull over.'

He eased the car over to the side of the road, the engine still running.

'I'll come with you, sir.'

'No, no, it's ok. I'm only going down there.' I pointed.

'Then I'll leave the engine running, sir.'

'Fine, whatever.'

I stepped out of the air-conditioned car into the blazing heat, and quickly took the ten steps into the narrow pedestrian street. The gap between buildings was covered with a random mixture of sheets and fabrics making a rough cover to block out the sun. In this shade customers could peruse the various market stalls in relative cool.

I passed a young boy selling fruit, an old wizened man selling perfumes, an old woman selling intricate necklaces and earrings. The smells were incredible. A mixture of spices, and perfume, and food, and sweat. It was an intense assault on the senses. Dappled light shooting in from the occasional hole or break in the covers; people calling from every stall, hawking their wares; the uneven ground. With a burst of adrenaline and a prickling down my spine, it dawned on me that this was my first experience of the real Argolis, the one lived in every day. A smile broke across my face, I could not help it. An old man, wrapped in black, standing in a doorway, leaning on a large stick, saw my smile and returned it. I laughed with joy. I looked down the narrow road to where the car waited on the main road, appearing and disappearing behind the energetic bodies. I could not see into the car through the tinted windows, but I threw Munir a reassuring wave.

I moved towards the man selling food, the smell guiding me towards the market's central crossroads. When I made it to him I saw that it was some kind of falafel paste, cooked into a flatbread on a hotplate instead of fried in little balls. I nodded to him and held up a single finger to demonstrate that I wanted one of whatever it was. He smiled and nodded. Not understanding the prices written in Arabic, or being able to ask, I passed him the second-smallest note I had on the assumption it would be enough. He smiled and placed it in a bum bag without giving me any change.

I waited for two minutes, then an older man appeared round the corner, holding a plate.

The man on the hotplate directed me to him. 'Go,'

he said in a low voice.

'Come,' the old man added in high-pitched response, leading me with the plate.

Just around the corner, on another market street there was a seating area of plastic tables and chairs. The old man placed the plate on a table and encouraged me to sit down. On the plate was the flatbread I had asked for, but with a large salad on the side. The old man tucked in my chair behind me and began to pour me a cup of coffee from a silver pot in a long and ostentatious arc. Not a drop landed on the table. He put the cup down by my plate, along with cutlery and olive oil, then patted my shoulder and retreated.

'Thank you,' I told him.

Halfway through my delicious meal, which I had drenched in delicious olive oil, I looked up to see that a well-groomed middle-aged man on a table diagonally opposite mine was studying me. He did not react with embarrassment when I saw him, he simply gave a closed and mirthless smile, stood up, and wandered away into the crowds.

By the end of my meal, I felt a sudden movement in my bowels. Perhaps I was not quite equipped to deal with the local food, or the water they had washed the salad in. I stood up quickly, looking around. The old man stepped out, looking at me with concerned eyes.

I smiled awkwardly, clutching my stomach.

'Bathroom?' he asked.

'Yes,' I replied with relief.

'Come, please,' he beckoned.

I followed him into the building, past the main kitchen, and into the back where a small but mercifully civilised toilet and sink were housed. There was no lock.

'I wait,' he told me, shutting the door behind me.

'Thank you,' I muttered.

When I had finished, I flushed, and washed my hands with water (there was no soap). Then I opened the door.

The old man was gone, replaced by two larger men. Before I had a chance to panic, a bag was over my head.

My hands were bound. I was dragged and pushed to a vehicle, then rocked around it as it drove for what seemed like hours. Then I was pulled, dragged, pushed into a room, hit if I was slow or resisted. They threw me to the ground. I found a corner and huddled into it, bringing my knees up to my chest. They bound my feet, I did not fight them.

They did not feed me for the rest of that day, or the night. Nor did they give me water. Nor take the bag off. My lips we stuck together; my tongue and throat burning. I clung to the small mercy that being so dehydrated and underfed meant I had not soiled myself. Light and dark reeled through the black fabric of the hood. Inside my inner world, the lights slowly died.

I was woken with a kick.

'Get up!'

I huddled further into the corner. Suddenly a man was over me, the bonds around my feet were cut, then the ones around my hands, and the hood pulled off. This all took seconds.

I recoiled from the brightness of the room. Something cold and wet was thrown in my face.

'Drink.'

It had only been a few splashes of water; the man was holding a bowl of it out to me. I drank the whole thing, panting.

'Up,' he commanded. Then he took me by the elbow and pulled me to my feet. He was twice my size.

'Walk.' He started leading me around the room, back and forth from wall to wall. It was morning of the next day, sunlight streaming through two high windows. 'Walk, walk,' he told me, repeating it every time I started to flag. We must have been walking for five minutes, back and forth, back and forth.

'Good.'

Finally, he opened the door and I was pushed down a corridor and into the hot sun. I squinted against the light, I could just about see orange desert between small huts, and could feel the sand on my face. We were no longer in the city. I thought I could hear the sea, but it could just be the blood in my ears.

I was led into another hut, where the big man opened a door and pushed me inside. Then he shut the door.

I was alone in an identical room to the one I had left. There was no real furniture, just some cushions on the floor and a low table. On the table was a spread of fruit, vegetables, dips, and breads. I ran to it and stuffed as much as I could into my mouth.

Five minutes later, once I had gorged myself, the door opened again. I instantly recoiled into the corner.

In strolled a handsome young man with long glossy hair and a neatly trimmed beard. He wore a pistol on his hip and a bandolier around his chest. He was carrying a wooden stool, which rather than sitting on he placed his foot on as though posing for a photograph. Behind him followed a woman with short hair and a Kalashnikov, she shut the door and sat crossed-legged on the floor with the AK-47 in her lap.

The man smiled at me. 'You've eaten, good.'

I stared at them out of my now feral eyes.

'I'm sorry for how they've treated you, Benjamin, they didn't know who you were. Then again, for your sake, maybe it's a good thing they didn't.'

He had a wry smile that did not put me at ease.

'My name is Bahadur. I'm sure you've heard of me. And I know who you are.'

I did not respond. He seemed disappointed.

'We're going to use you as a hostage for an exchange. I have no desire to mistreat you. You will be well looked after. But... don't try to escape. My men aren't all as civilised as I am.'

He glanced at the food, then had a brainwave and darted out of the room. He returned a minute later with a small bowl of raspberries that he added to the table.

'I bet you haven't had these in a while,' he added with excitement as he plucked one from the bowl for himself. 'They've been frozen of course, can't grow them here.' He threw the raspberry in his mouth. 'I love these damn things.'

I took one and put it in my mouth, allowing it to moisten my throat before I croaked: 'You developed a taste for them whilst you were studying in England?'

His wry smile reappeared. 'Nice try, Ben, but I studied at the university here in Argolis. And don't think you're surreptitiously gathering any useful information about me. The powers that be know exactly who I am.' He popped another one in his mouth. 'They even know I like raspberries.'

I helped myself to more, they were the sweetest thing on the table and my body needed the sugar.

'How long are you going to keep me here?' I asked.

'No longer than necessary.'

'What are you trading me for, another prisoner?'

He scoffed. 'No, my men are willing to die for the cause. I'm trading you for something far more important.'

'What makes you think I'm worth anything to them?'

'You are to the king, Ben.'

'Really?'

He tutted and shook his head like a teacher. 'Don't insult us both. We know all about you: you're The Jew.'

'Is that right? How come you know so much about me?'

'Let's just say we have our sources.' He smiled. 'Yes, you're worth a lot to him, which means your worth a lot to us.'

I sighed. 'What is it you want that's so important?'

'Free and fair elections. Just at the community level, mind. Open for anyone to stand, and for anyone over the age of fourteen to vote.'

'There are already community elections.'

He scoffed again. 'What, the ones where every candidate has to be approved by the government, where only men over the age of eighteen can vote? What would you call that in your country?'

'As soon as you arrange the deal they'll just send the army to wipe you out, best to let me go now.'

'I think we'll be all right.'

'How many men have you got on your side?'

He smiled. 'I think we'll be all right.'

'Fine. And once you give me up, what's there to stop them going back on their word?'

He smiled yet again, everything I said seemed to amuse him. 'Because we won't release you until the election has been held.'

The bottom fell out of my stomach. I felt despair. Then I felt angry, as though nothing mattered. If they were not going to let me go today then what difference did it make whether they let me go at all.

'You're a fool,' I told him.

That did not amuse him. 'Excuse me?'

'You're giving them a media victory.'

'Oh, a *media* victory?'

'Yes!' I shouted, my throat still raw. 'Now they get to paint democracy as the will of violent guerrillas. To everyone else you're no different to those who attacked the oil fields.'

His laugh was deep in his throat now. He bit his lip. 'I see. And what exactly are we supposed to do in the meantime, just wait for the king to pull democracy out of his arse?'

'Yes!'

He laughed even louder. 'When!?'

'When...' I clenched my fists, 'when it's the right time.'

'Oh, you mean when the current crisis is resolved

and the oil fields are fixed back up to full capacity? When the terrorists have been defeated? When the situation in the Gulf de-escalates?' He stood up, leaning over the table towards me. 'When the ulama can be convinced to meet halfway? When the economy is strong enough? Once the king has had a chance get things done!?' He stood back up straight, taking a step back. 'I've heard all these excuses before, Mr Hollow, I worked in the government. Just like you. But unlike you I couldn't square my conscience. I couldn't work for a dictator.'

'He's not a dictator.'

'Why, because he calls himself a king?' He turned away.

'He doesn't kidnap people.'

'You're a rat,' the woman hissed. She spat at me.

'Oh, leave him, Sara,' he told her with resignation.

But a fire burned in her eyes. 'Do you know how many times I've been raped?' she continued. 'Neither do I. By soldiers. By police. By my husband. And what can I do? In law I have no more rights than the television he slaps when it doesn't work. There are no women in your world, are there? In your gold corridors?' She looked at me with contempt. 'You hadn't even noticed.'

I wanted to shout. To scream. But I knew she was right. But I also knew he was wrong.

'You worked in the government?' I asked him.

He was pacing. 'Yes, I worked for them. Back then I believed in it all.' He stopped and closed his eyes, listening.

I listened too. I could definitely hear the sea, but nothing more.

'This place,' he said, eyes still closed, 'this little village, is no different to the one al-Abu grew up in, you know. Untouched, I find it incredible. You can't even see the city from here. Out here is where he dreamed of Argolis as a boy, and one day every schoolboy would be taught to share that dream.' He opened his eyes. 'Do you know what woke me up?'

I shrugged.

'It was the killing. You know, every successive dictator starts with a purge. When you have that much power there are always people looking to wrestle it from you. Plotting, scheming, conspiring. The transition may be smooth on the surface, but there is always a struggle going on. A game of musical chairs.'

He stopped pacing and put his foot back on the stool. 'In 1947, once al-Abu had united the tribes and used them to drive out the British, he welcomed the tribal leaders to the old imperial palace to discuss their share in the new country. He treated them to the best food from the British stores, and once they had filled their bellies his guards took out their Kalashnikovs and blew them all to shreds. There were to be no shares in his country. It was one of the greatest mistakes Abdullah made, not to kill his younger brothers as soon as he took the throne. He had to wait for them to try and kill him instead. I don't advocate fratricide, of course, but if you're going to be a dictator you have to *be* a dictator. You can't be half-tyrant. But he learnt his lesson, so, after their attempted coup he had his surviving brothers killed or imprisoned, and executed those in military that had aided them. His reign continued unchallenged for forty years.'

He started moving again, stopping to bask with closed eyes in the shaft of sunlight coming through the one high window. 'When I joined the government we had been taught that our country ran so smoothly, was advancing so quickly, because it did not have any of the pesky bureaucracy and corruption that plagued Western so-called democracies. Then, one day, we had to decide whether or not to execute a man for blasphemy, on the word of the ulama. I did some digging, and found that the man was a journalist, and that his "blasphemy" was that he had exposed some of the ulama's financial irregularities. I told Daniel al-Hadi, and he told me that the man's life was not important, what was important was keeping the ulama happy. That's what they always tell you: we must allow corruption because the alternative will be somehow worse. That's when I realised it was all a lie. Everything the country was built on. Every word that came out of their mouths. And everyone knows it. Daniel knew it. I knew it. The king new it. Even the man selling falafel in the street knows it. But we all pretend, because we have no truth anymore. We wouldn't know the truth if we saw it sitting in front of us.'

I watched his closed eyes. 'And now you're killing people to stop the killing.'

He opened them and smiled. 'One of life's little ironies, I suppose.'

'Why do they call you the Turk?'

He turned away, pacing again. 'Oh, that's Daniel's work. They call me that because it's foreign, it makes people think I'm just some outsider trying to cause trouble. No honest Argolisian would want to overthrow the king.'

'What makes you think it was Daniel?'

He stopped pacing. 'I don't think, I know: he was the only one who knew my mother was Turkish. You see, that's how he works, he is a true master of lies. He knows that, like a pearl, every great lie, the strong ones that really last, have just a grain of truth at the centre.'

He would hate to hear it, but he reminded me of Amal. Less graceful, more confident, but idealistic, and passionate.

I started slowly, keeping my voice calm and genuine,

appealing to them: 'The king, my friend, he wants democracy, he really does. He wants everything you want. Both of you. But if even he can't get it, what hope do you have?'

He turned back to face me, his hand reflexively on his gun handle. 'What would you do?'

'Work together.'

He laughed. 'The king, and the rebels, together? How is that going to work?'

'Badly, at first. But you want the same things. And you can't do it alone. Every war ends with people talking, so let's just skip the war part, and get round the table. I actually think he'd be happy.'

'Daniel al-Hadi would never allow it,' the woman mocked.

'Daniel al-Hadi works for the king,' I replied sharply.

He looked up from the table, into my eyes. His fingers were playing with his bottom lip.

She looked at him. 'Don't be stupid, we have him, we can get community elections.'

I was looking him dead in the eyes. I jokingly scoffed at her idea, raising my eyebrows and shrugging my shoulders: community elections were small fry. One side of his mouth curled up in that wry smile.

There was a sudden rising scream like the screech of a kettle, and then my ears exploded and I felt the impact of the stone wall on my back. The air rang, dust scattered, gunshots cracked around my head. Blood ran into my eyes. The room was gone. I was huddled in a corner which was all that was left of the building.

9

Mighty Despair

THE BLOOD DRIED, sealing my right eye shut, picking up the dust and sand from the air. I was rolled onto a stretcher, put in the back of an ambulance, a breathing mask over my face. When I woke I was in a concrete cell, with no light but that which bled around the door. I had the smothered feeling of being underground.

I heard screams, both men's and women's, though the wall by the bucket I urinated in; pleasurable sounds of intercourse, like pornography, through the wall by my bed. As I laid there a wet patch began to form on the ceiling above my head until it pursed into single drip that fell towards my eyes, but I did not feel it.

The door unlocked with a deafening clang and I was dragged from the cell, down a concrete corridor, and into an interrogation room. I was placed into a nailed-down metal chair and handcuffed to the scarred wooden table. I was alone. A strip light hummed above, throwing a sickly urine-coloured glow onto a flat reel-to-reel tape recorder.

From the shadows beyond the light-haze a man in a grey suit emerged holding a file in green card. As he sat down into the chair opposite, my heart leapt to see who it was.

'Daniel,' I almost cried.

He opened the file and started to read it with great interest. I felt like a ghost.

'Daniel!'

He tutted at something in the file. Still apparently oblivious.

I could not reach out to shake him so I filled my lungs and I blew at his papers. They rippled and slid and he had to stop one sailing off the desk. He was frozen now, but the spell had been broken. He looked up at my face, deep into my welling eyes. Nothing stirred in his. Then he reached over and pressed a button on the tape recorder and the reels slowly revolved with a faint whine.

'Beginning interview with prisoner 5 4 7 2—'

'What the hell is this!?' I shouted over him.

He started again: 'Beginning interview with prisoner 5 4 7—'

'Benedict—' I screamed, but there was a loud *click* and the reels stopped.

He withdrew his finger from the button and placed them calmly interlinked on the table. After a minute he took a pencil and notebook from his inside pocket and placed them on the desk, calmly interlinking his hands again.

Once we had both been silent for two minutes he asked a question: 'How long have you been working with the rebels?'

I laughed.

He did not.

'You're serious?' I asked.

He did not answer.

'Of course you're not serious. This is all part of the game.'

'What game?' He asked in that practiced form of non-pressuring interest that therapists and psychiatrists master.

I did not answer.

'Is this a game to you?' he probed.

I tilted my head in disappointment. If my hands were free I could have strangled him.

'How long have your government been aiding the rebels?'

'How the hell would I know?'

'So you don't deny it.' He wrote a short sentence in the notebook.

I pushed my tongue around my mouth, nodding in

disbelief, chuckling to myself.

'You find it amusing?'

'I find *you* amusing,' I told him.

A small smile curled his lip, then died. 'How long have you been supplying information to the British government?'

I huffed.

'No?'

'No,' I stated.

He turned a sheet in the file as though checking something, then looked back up at me. 'You've supplied information to the British government on at least one confirmed occasion.'

'Have I really?' I asked sarcastically.

'Yes, you have. It's no secret, you're good friends with the man.'

'And who's that?'

He said each word distinctly, relishing them. 'Mark. Lowden.'

I swallowed, feeling my Adam's apple slipping down my throat.

'Handsome, dashing, Scottish geological engineer, and known MI6 operative. We've had him on our books for quite some time, wondering who he would make a play for. And then you came along, swimming right into his cove. He must not have believed his luck: here was a young, ignorant, naïve virgin, plucked from obscurity and placed in the highest echelons of government. A man with the king's ear. A man whose ear the king has. And what the king tells you, you tell him. Very tidy.'

'You're lying.' I did not know what else to try.

He shook his head calmly, genuinely. 'No.'

I went to itch my prickly chin, but my hands could only move an inch from the table leg.

I glanced up at him and pushed out a long, slow breath. 'Look, Daniel...' I stuttered, halting, 'if it's true, if he's a spy, then maybe he *was* trying to...' I lost the words.

'Pump you?' he asked. 'Develop you as a source?'

'Yes. But I never told him anything.'

'Then what did you tell him, the night of the oil field attack, the night you wanted to speak to the king *so* badly.'

'He told me they had people working out there. That they needed to know whether or not to send a rescue mission.'

'A rescue mission? A geological survey company?'

'Yes.'

'Is that what you really thought?'

'I *wasn't* thinking. But I didn't tell him anything important.'

'Military activity?'

'It couldn't possibly be valuable to them.'

'Perhaps, this time. How much easier it would be

next time to ask for something more. It's how these things work.'

'I didn't know that. I wasn't thinking.'

He leaned back in his chair. 'So, that's the choice I have, is it? Do I believe you're a spy, or a moron?'

'Please, Daniel.'

He just raised his eyebrows.

'Please,' I begged.

'Please, what? Please believe I'm an idiot?'

I just stared.

'No, Ben, I don't believe you're stupid. In fact, I think you're very clever indeed.' He closed the notebook and stood up. 'We'll continue this tomorrow, you might want to consider telling the truth.'

'No!' I screamed.

He looked at me like something that had crawled onto his shoe.

'I want to see the king!'

'The king, as you know, is in Doha.'

'And what is he going to do when he hears about this!? He'll have you hanged!'

'When he hears about *what*? He has yet to be informed about today's military action. *I* will inform him.'

'And what happened to me!?'

'You disappeared into a market street in the middle of the city, your driver witnessed it, you were never seen again. One of life's little mysteries, I suppose. He'll soon get over you. I might buy him a puppy.'

'This is all because I told you to fuck off, isn't it!? Because I argued with you. I met your friend yesterday: Bahadur. It sounds like there wasn't any love lost between you. It must really cut you up that he betrayed you like that, but I bet what really rankles is that he argued with you. He didn't treat your wisdom with the reverence it deserves. Does it still upset you?' I thought if I could make him angry I could keep him in the room.

He left a two-second pause. 'Not anymore.' I felt the chill in his voice down my spine.

'You're nothing but a leech.'

'Is that what you think I am? A bloodsucker. Or just a showman? A sycophant, or the puppet master? Wise political operator, or intransigent snob?'

He stood there a moment, one finger on the table, his face just above the line of light.

'I'm going to tell you what I do to prisoners who won't tell the truth, and then you can decide what you think of me.' He left another pause, filled only by the hum of the light. 'When they go back to their cells I let them sleep, naturally, no sedatives. Then the doctors sneak in and they give them an anaesthetic. Then we remove just one small part of them. We always start with a thumb. When they wake up, it's gone. We interrogate them again, and if they still won't tell the truth, we go in the next night, and we take something else. Not always something visible. A metatarsal perhaps. And the same on the third night. And the forth night. On the fifth night, we don't take anything at all, nor on the sixth, nor the seventh. But they still look, desperately, clawing at themselves with thumb-less hands. You see, under physical pain a man will say almost anything to make it stop. Horror is the way to loosen a man's tongue.' He smiled. 'If he still has one.'

'I've told you the truth!'

'Please, Ben, you're not doing yourself any favours by lying to me.'

'I've told you the truth!'

He moved to the door, his hand on the knob.

'Wait! I did it! I did it, ok!?'

'What?' He did not even turn to face me.

'I work for MI6, I'm a spy, I want to bring down the government by arming the rebels.'

'What was the plan?'

I tried to think. 'I don't know.'

'Not good enough.' He turned the handle.

'Please, I don't know!' I screamed. 'I'm just a pawn! A fool. I've been used. I'm an idiot.' I started to cry, snot running down my face and over my lips. 'I don't belong here,' I whimpered. 'I don't belong here.'

I sat hunched over, sobbing, my stomach twitching and chest tightening.

'I believe you,' he whispered.

I tried to look up but could not see through my streaming eyes.

'Someone will come and get you in a minute, you'll be checked out by our doctors and given some clean clothes, you'll probably stay in the hospital for a few days. Then you will be free to go back to your house.'

'I'll go back to England, you'll never see me again.'

'I understand, of course, but I hope you'll consider staying.'

I tried to blink the tears away.

'The king needs you.'

I felt more confused than ever.

'Whatever you think of me, Ben, I'm loyal. And I think so are you.'

Part IV

Nothing beside remains. Round the decay
Of that colossal Wreck, boundless and bare
The lone and level sands stretch far away."

Ozymandias, Percy Bysshe Shelley

10

Cold Command

THEY KEPT ME IN a hospital for five days. Clean, white sheets, and decent food. A doctor checked on me the first day, and after that I only saw nurses. They were very kind. On the sixth day they called for Munir to drive me home.

'I'm so sorry, sir, this is my fault,' he told me as we cruised down the silent tarmac away from the city and towards the sand dunes on the horizon.

'No, it isn't,' I told him, 'It's mine.'

When we arrived at the complex a small crowd of residents and servants had gathered. As I limped from the car they applauded.

Abderrazzaq had run me a bath, and food was being prepared. I told him to cancel the food, or enjoy it himself, and said thank you for the bath. I sat in it until it was cold, then laid in my bed and cried myself to sleep.

✦

The next morning I slept in late, then Munir drove me to the palace, cruising down the tarmac boulevard. As we approached the government sector the number of people on the pavements gradually increased, each head turning at the sight of the black Mercedes. As we got closer to the palace people spat silent words in our direction. Within sight of the gates and iron-spiked walls, men started walking alongside the car, trying to stare in through the tinted glass. At the gates a few protesters were shouting to the distant windows. When they saw us approach they turned their fire on us, banging on the car and trying the door handles. In my traumatised state it was terrifying, but we were soon inside and safely behind bars.

I left Munir and climbed the steps through the shout-filled air. I found Amal standing in one of the upstairs staterooms, at a window that had a view over the gates and walls, and the crowd beyond. The carpet was purple and plush, the walls cream, the ceiling sculpted. Every point and protrusion was tipped with gold. Impractical gold-edged chaise lounges occupied the centre, more gilded furniture dotted the outskirts.

'Ben!' he cried with joy, but tinged with exhaustion. 'How are you?' He gave me a strong embrace.

'Where's Daniel, we need to talk?' I stammered.

'I can send for him if you want.'

'No, I mean, where is he because *we* need to talk. Alone. Before the audience.'

He saw I was serious. 'Sure. Ok, now. We can talk now.'

'You're not expecting anyone? No one is going to burst in with something for you to sign?'

He touched my elbow. 'No. What is it?'

I tried to calm my breathing. I was aware I was twitching. 'How was Doha?'

A frown appeared too easily on his once-untouched face. 'Not good. We can't borrow any more from our neighbours.'

'What about the Chinese?'

'Bad news there too, I'm afraid. The country is considered too unstable at the moment to be a sound investment.'

'Europe?'

'No. A matter of principle.'

'America?'

He raised his eyebrows and turned back to the window. 'There's only one thing they want.'

'Then give it to them.'

'I will not destroy my father's legacy.'

'Since when have you cared about your father's legacy?' I blurted incredulously.

'Since I've sat on his throne.'

I held my jaw tight. 'Sell them back their shares, save your people.' I gestured to the crowds.

'I'd be betraying them. It's their oil, I won't give it back to the Americans.'

'Your people are struggling to buy bread and water. Are you going to tell them to drink the oil?'

He did not answer, glaring at me with white eyes.

'Amal, this place is rotten. I didn't see it when I arrived, I didn't see it for a long time. You think the world smells of fresh paint, but it's just a backdrop, and behind it the place is ready to crumble. It looks right from where you are, but move just a little and the illusion is obvious. I've seen it.'

'I think you need some rest, Ben, you've been through a lot.'

'We need to get out of here, far, far away. You need to resign. You need to announce elections. You need to start the process now. Today.'

He smiled in disbelief. 'You think *this* is the right time?'

'Yes.'

'Now? You really think *now* is the time?'

'Yes.'

He scoffed. 'What about that list? What about all the things we were going to do whilst we had the chance?'

'Bin it. It was a dream.'

He looked at me. He was disappointed with what he saw.

'If not now, when?' I asked.

'I don't know,' he stated defiantly. 'Not now. We're in the middle of a crisis. Get them to vote tomorrow, who do you think they'll elect? They're scared, they're angry—'

'Yes!'

'—who will they turn to? We need the economy to be booming, we need people to be happy, or they'll elect some backwards Ayatollah! They'll set this country back a thousand years!' He calmed himself. 'No, Ben, now is not the time.'

'It's always been the time.' I almost whispered it.

He sighed. 'Maybe you should go home.'

'I feel fine.'

'I mean *home*, Ben. England. Croydon. Your mother.'

'Why would you say that to me?'

'You've done your summer work experience, haven't you? Go get your foreign office job. Wasn't that what this was all about?'

'How can you not know?'

He stared at me with wet eyes, face quivering, but holding it together.

'Slip out the back door with me. Right now. We'll get in my car, we'll just drive. Drive and drive.'

He looked up at the lights, face sagging, eyes welling, and then clenched tightly, glistening at the edges. 'I can't,' he breathed, eyes open again, pleading silently with me.

The door opened sharply. We both jumped out of our skin.

'There they are,' announced Daniel with relief, hurrying into the room, followed closely by the General and the chief of police.

'We may as well stay in here now that we're all together,' Daniel suggested.

Amal nodded to avoid speaking.

'Waa'il, can you get them to bring in some coffee?'

The chief dutifully padded out the door.

The general slapped me on the shoulder. 'I'm glad to see you're all right. Next time don't go wandering off, you might not be so lucky.'

'They'll bring it in a second,' the chief said as he returned to what was now a loose huddle, standing in the middle of the stateroom.

'First of all,' Daniel handed a file to each of us, 'here is the report on the military action that took place whilst you were away. But the headline news is that the general's men equipped themselves as well as ever, and thanks to our intelligence, the rebels have now been thoroughly decapitated.'

'Here, here,' added the general.

'The more pressing matter is the issue of further borrowing. Since we are unable to secure further investment in our current situation we will of course have to increase the rate of the Repair Tax.'

'You can't take any more away from these people,' I protested.

They all responded uncomfortably to the emotion in my voice.

Ignoring me, Amal spoke gently. 'How high will the tax have to go?'

'I suggest seventy percent.'

'Is there a way to make it more progressive?'

'As you know, a lot of the country's wealth exists outside the tax system, both in the hands of immigrants and in property and other overseas investment.'

'You mean embezzlement,' I drawled.

Daniel's nostrils flared.

'Government employees funnelling government money into shell companies, foreign property, and other untaxable assets. You're all happy to let that money trickle out until you want to pull it back.'

The chief shifted his feet uncomfortably. Daniel and the general stayed rooted to the spot.

'Not that I need to tell you lot, it's *your* corrupt fortunes I'm talking about.'

'You're so innocent as always, Mr Hollow,' Daniel sneered. 'Some might call arranging meetings with the king for your friends and fellow countrymen, just because they ask you in the right language "corruption". But then, you wouldn't do *that*, would you?... Which reminds me, I have cancelled your dinner invitation to a certain ex-Prime Minister with a—shall we say—*nuanced* reputation in this part of the world. That's not how we do things here.'

'Maybe you're right: for it to be corruption it has to go against the established system. Here, embezzlement, fraud, and oligarchy *is* the system. And now it's going to impoverish your people.'

'There is no choice, Mr Hollow, we have no other viable funding streams.'

'None that the king will accept.'

'That being the case, we must pursue the only alternative. He is our king.'

'Not mine.'

I turned away before they had time to look appalled, and moved to the window. Their voices became small, distant things.

'There'll be more protests,' the chief mumbled.

'Without the rebels to organise them, they won't be any threat.'

'My own men are just as unhappy; is there nothing we can do?'

'Perhaps exceptions could be made for essential government workers. A two-tier system.'

'Yes, that would do. Then my men, as police officers, would be one of those exceptions?'

'Of course.'

'Yes, that will do fine.'

'What about *my* men, they won't accept police getting paid and them getting shafted.'

'We cannot exempt every soldier; they represent too large a percentage of government employees.'

'Yes, but not too large a percentage of government payroll. My men earn half what one of your junior civil servants earns.'

'We could perhaps make an exception for officers.'

'That will do for now.'

'Then we are agreed. I will prepare a proposal for next week. Next on today's agenda is the state dinner for the delegation from Yemen. I suggest we postpone the entire visit; we should not be antagonising our Saudi neighbours at this time. And we don't want to be seen to be feathering our own nests.'

I was looking through the glass to the crowd below. There were perhaps only a hundred of them, but more were trickling down the roads towards the palace gates, half of them just curious. The ones at the gates, closest to the guards, were all men, shouting, gesticulating. One brandished his young daughter, shouting at a guard and holding up the girl's thin wrist. She wore a plain blue dress and clung to his trouser leg with her free hand.

Another of the men had a frightened boy huddled between his legs.

Behind the angry men were the younger and older men. The younger men shouting over shoulders, jostling to be nearer the front. The older were either watching silently or praying with their arms raised to the heavens. Behind them women stood, most of them with children clinging to their arms or on their shoulders. One young woman without a headscarf broke through the ranks of men to join those at the gates, joining in the shouting, spraying saliva as she screamed at the guards.

Presently, some guards appeared with baskets of bread and started to throw loaves one at a time into the crowd. The first person to catch one hugged it to their breast and ran as fast as they could out of the crowd and away. The next few spirited it away into their clothes and raised their hands, hoping for more. After a dozen had been distributed, the next man to catch one launched it back at the guards with a loud cry. Inspired, another person took theirs from their robes and threw it over the heads of the crowd and over the gate. Then there was another, and another, until everyone who had received a loaf had thrown it back.

The crowd advanced as one to the gates, hands on the iron bars. They began pushing and pulling, rattling the metal. Guards tried desperately to uncoil fingers, but every time they peeled a hand from the iron another took its place. They started smashing their rifle butts on the white knuckles, but there were too many to stop.

'Look on your Works,' I called to the others.

The doors to the stateroom burst apart and the Chief of the Palace Guard jogged into the room.

'Your Majesty, we need to get you to safety.'

'What's happening?' Daniel demanded.

'The crowds, sir, we can't control them. In a minute they'll be climbing the walls.'

'You *must* control them,' Daniel ordered.

'How, sir?'

'Fire over their heads,' the general suggested.

I leaped from the window. 'God, no! That will make things worse!'

Daniel turned to Amal. 'We have no choice.'

'Don't listen to them,' I begged. 'You need to de-escalate the situation, not escalate it further.'

Amal turned to the police chief, who, after a moment of indecision, nodded feebly.

'You do this, you're no better than your father!' I screamed.

He turned to the chief of the guard. 'Do it.'

I ran back to the window. The electric gate was now tilted at an angle, half out of its track. Within seconds the order had got down to the guards and one fired his automatic rifle into the air. The crowds scrambled from the bars, tripping and falling as they tried to get away. Most were busy scattering but as a few spun back up from the ground they lobbed a stone in the direction of the guards. Two or three more at the back were busy doing the same but with clearer aim. A few rocks clanged off the metal of the gate and the guards flinched and ducked. Two more guards fired their rifles into the air. Ten more people threw stones. One struck a guard in the head, knocking his hat off, and sending him to the ground. The man who had thrown it raised his arms in celebration. There was the crack of a single gunshot and he was on the floor. There were screams, more stones thrown, more shots fired into the crowd. This time they really ran, leaving behind half a dozen bodies. Amongst the swirling dust the little girl still clung to the trouser leg of her now deceased father.

11

A Shattered Visage

THE GUARDS TRIED desperately to realign the electric gate in its track, but the protesters had damaged it too severely. One corner was tilted in towards the complex, leaving a gap large enough to enter through. The rest of the guards reloaded their rifles. They snapped into formation to aim them at a man approaching the gate. The man held his open hands above his head and continued to approach the girl clinging to her dead father. He peeled her from the body and ran away with her tucked in his arms.

'That gate won't hold,' the general stated, buttoning up his uniform to its fullest splendour. 'I'll return with a battalion of my men to secure the complex.'

'Return?' the police chief asked. 'Perhaps I better go with you.'

'No, you'll need to coordinate the palace guard, these

useless fucks will benefit from your experience.'

The chief nodded reluctantly and headed out of the room.

Amal and Daniel were standing by the window, examining the defensive efforts. 'I don't think they'll be able to open the gate for your car,' Daniel mused.

'I'll get out the back way,' the general replied matter-of-factly.

It was just the two of us standing by the door now. He leaned in towards me.

'Whilst I have the chance, I just want to say how much I've appreciated having you here these last few months.'

I was shocked.

'It's been a pleasure, Benjamin.' He held out his hand.

I shook it, still in a daze. Then he was gone.

I drifted back to the window. Daniel and Amal were watching over the gate. Daniel turned as I approached, shocked to find me the only person in the room.

'Where is the chief of the guard?' His voice contained palpable concern.

'Where do you think? His men just killed unarmed protesters.'

'They were armed with rocks!' he snapped, before returning to the subject: 'He needs to get the king to safety.'

We looked back over the approach to the gates. The streets were empty except for a dog sniffing at one of the bodies. His ears pricked and he raised his nose from the man's armpit. He listened, looked down the road behind him, then shot off down an alley. On the sides of buildings shadows danced, then heads appeared marching, above the heads were raised Kalashnikovs, pistols, and improvised clubs.

The first shots caught the guards unprepared, three hit the ground, hats rolling. Shots were fired back but the sheer force of fifty angry men trampled the gate. The guards scattered. Some retreated orderly up the steps towards the palace, alternately laying covering fire. Others ran wildly towards the parked cars and were promptly shot in the back, arching and spinning as they fell.

'Quickly!' shouted the chief of the guard from the doorway.

We three ran from the window, across the stateroom, through the cream and gold doors, onto the red-carpeted landing at the top of the main stairs, where a huddle of guards was waiting to envelop us. Some guards from outside were already on the stairs, they caught bullets as our feet scrabbled on the carpet, gaping down at the invaders already flooding into the main entrance hall, seeing them chase the guards up, and spinning to run across the vast landing and down the nearest corridor.

We left two of our huddle firing behind us down the stairs. As we reached the end of the corridor and turned a corner I caught a snapshot of their bodies lying on the carpet.

We ran through a door, down three narrow flights of stairs lit only with red bulbs, into a concrete corridor, and towards a door opened into the passageway, where the chief of police beckoned us on. He lurched forward and fell flat on his face, leaving four small bullet holes in the door behind him. We stopped to spin back just as a man with a Kalashnikov charged into the open door, slamming it shut with a leap over the body and storming towards us.

We pumped our legs back up the red-lit narrow stairs, our last two guards staying to lay covering fire. We soon heard footsteps charging up the stairs behind us. As we opened the door at the top we emerged into a crossroads. Three armed invaders in the path ahead raised their guns and we split instinctively. Daniel and the chief of the guard ran into the corridor on their right. Amal and I ran left. We heard deafening shots from various weapons as we sprinted down the short corridor, took another left, lunged through a door, down one flight of stairs, into another corridor, down a slightly sloped passageway, and through a metal door.

The corridors had changed from gold carpeted boulevards to narrow bare stone passageways. We were in the servants' area.

We ran past a small kitchen and store room, broom cupboards and piles of dirty linen. These corridors were empty but windowless and labyrinthine. Lost, without guards or weapons, we both ran instinctively for the toilets by the kitchen, into a cubicle, and locked the door.

Amal was on the closed lid of the seat, I was at his feet, braced between the two walls. A single frosted, unopening window behind his head let some grey light in to reflect off the shabby white tiles and grotty bathroom sealant. We sat panting for at least two minutes, lactic acid filling our throats, getting the shakes when feeling returned to our fingers.

Amal pulled out a mobile phone when he could speak again. 'The general won't be long, I'll tell him where to find us.' He dialled the number and held the phone to his ear.

Terror was driven through me like a spike. 'NO, WAIT!' I screamed and snatched the phone from his ear, ending the call.

Amal looked almost as scared, but it gave way to confusion and anger.

I whispered, almost to myself: 'He's not coming back here to save you. He's coming to kill you.'

He smiled, amused by the ridiculous idea, but again

it evolved into anger. 'What's wrong with you?'

I continued to think out loud: 'How could I be so stupid? *"Benjamin"*. When I first met the general he got my name wrong, he did it again just now. Bahadur did the same. He did the same because he got his information from the general, although he probably didn't know it. He probably communicated with some Lieutenant-Colonel, some officer both high and low enough to be believable. That's what he meant when I asked him how many men he had on his side.'

'The general's not working with the rebels, his men killed Bahadur saving your life.'

'That was probably part of his plan. In fact, of course it was. He didn't care about them, he was just using them to destabilise the country. *He* had your brother killed. Your brother was too reliable, too steady to make this crisis possible. He's been biding his time since, waiting patiently. Manoeuvring. Your father let him place his men one-to-one with the police at every checkpoint, on every patrol. Now, when he gives the order, if he hasn't already, they can take control of the city. And whilst you've been starving the people, cutting the pay of your own guards, he's been selling his fortune to keep his men well paid and loyal. He'll storm the palace only to find you conveniently shot. He'll blame you for ordering the guards to fire on the protesters. He'll blame me too, paint me as a Jewish Rasputin. With no direct heir to the throne, he'll seize control, only temporarily of course, "a period of transition". Then he'll do what all dictators do: promise freedom and deliver slavery.'

Amal scoffed, but it was just a pathetic attempt to convince himself it was not true. The mocking smile soon died, replaced with a haughty intake of breath that puffed up his chest. 'The people would never follow a man like him.'

'Born poor in the coastal communities, just an ordinary man, enlisting in the army at the bottom rung, working hard, earning his way up to officer class, all the way to the top, finally, selflessly, freeing his people from an oppressive regime? It's a familiar story. It may even be destiny.'

He still did not believe me. He opened his mouth to speak just as the cubicle door thudded gently in a breeze. There was a creak from the outside door. We froze solid.

Footsteps smacked quietly on the damp vinyl floor. They squelched as they stopped. A zip was undone, then the tinkling of urine on porcelain drifted under the centimetre gap at the bottom of the dark wooden door to our cubicle. It stopped, the zip was pulled back up, and footsteps padded over to the sink. The tap ran, then stopped. But the footsteps did not move again. I could feel my pulse throbbing in my ears.

They squeaked towards us, stopping just beyond our

door. The handle rattled, twisted, the wood strained against the bolt. The handle was released. I could see two pools of shadow in the tiny centimetre gap above the floor. We both held our hands to our mouths, suffocating ourselves. Then came the sound that stopped my heart: the *ker-chunk* of a cocked gun.

I felt I could see the man there, seeing through the door. He stood with his legs firmly apart, ready for the recoil from the Kalashnikov he aimed just level with Amal's chest. It would spray a hail of bullets through the door, spitting fire and splinters into my eyes, followed by blood and dust and my dead friend's body slumped on mine.

Instead the pools of shadow had gone. There was another gentle creak as the corridor door softly shut.

We pushed air back out of our lungs, then sucked in deep, shivering breaths. Amal looked down at me from the throne.

'I don't suppose that offer you made is still available?' he asked with a sad smile.

'It is, if we can get out of here alive.' How that was possible I had no idea.

I was still holding Amal's phone. I tried calling the only person I could think of. He did not answer first time, I had to call again.

'Hello?' he answered a little too casually.

'It's Ben.'

'Ben! Where are you?'

'The palace.'

'My god! Are you all right?' His concern sounded genuine.

'Mark, I need your help.'

'*My* help?'

'I know who you are—who you work for—who you *really* work for.'

I heard the start of a dismissing laugh.

'Don't insult me by lying.'

There was a sigh, then silence. I held it, the ball was in his court. 'I think you're mistaken—' he heard me start to huff, '—about how things might work. I *am* a geological engineer.'

'Just with a side hustle in espionage.'

'Ben...' there came that dismissing laugh, 'if that were true then you would be helping your own country. What do you expect me to say?'

'"I owe you, Ben, for tricking you. Let me help you."'

He sighed again, disdainful. 'Assuming, for the moment, that you are *not* mistaken, what do you think I can do?'

'I am a British citizen, I am hiding in a toilet, with the king, the internationally recognised leader of this country, whilst Kalashnikov-wielding revolutionaries sweep the palace trying to kill us. Send the fucking SAS!'

'Even if I had the power to do that, the nearest British army bases are in Iraq and Afghanistan, call the Argolisian army.'

'They're too busy right now committing a coup.'

There was a beat of silence. 'Are you serious?'

I did not answer, I would not let him use me again.

'I'm sorry, Ben, I can't help you. I have to go.'

'No, Mark! No! You owe me!'

'I'm sorry.' He hung up.

I would have punched the tiles if I was the type. Amal gave a me a commiserating smile. It was sickly, that smile, so pitiful. *Cheer up*, it said, *better luck next time*. I was not going to let that smile be the end of this, this was not coming last at school sports day.

'We have to leave whilst the place is still in chaos.' I croaked. 'When Othman returns the first thing he'll do is lock the complex down.' I searched today's conversations for anything useful. 'He said he was going to leave by the back way. What did he mean?'

'I don't know.'

'Think!'

'I suppose... there's a tunnel, it runs underground for two hundred metres and comes up into a little guardhouse outside the walls. But it's not been used for years.'

'Where's the entrance?'

'The west wing, in the audience chamber.'

'Where are we now?'

'The east wing, about as far away as possible.'

'What else is in the east wing?'

'Just the servants' area, and my sister's residence above us.'

'Is she up there!?'

'They're skiing in Switzerland.'

'She has incredible luck.' I smiled in disbelief. I felt like laughing or crying, I did not know which. I returned to the more pressing issue: 'Everyone is looking for you, we have to get to the west side unseen,' I thought some more. 'Upstairs, in your sister's rooms, she has veils and face scarves?'

'Of course.'

'Then there's only one thing for it. Do you know the quickest way there?'

'When my brother and I were little we used to play hide and seek for hours, I know every corner of this building. Back then those were my aunt's rooms.'

'Ok, so I'm going to unlock this door, then you're going to run as fast as you can to your sister's rooms, and I'll be right behind you.'

He barely nodded. I took three long, deep breaths and reached for the lock. He grabbed my hand to stop me.

'Ben...' he whispered.

I looked in terror at him.

'Thank you.'

I could not speak to respond, so I nodded, then I reached for the lock.

I ran out into the toilets, he darted past me to the main door, sneaked it open an inch, looked for a second, and ran. I could barely keep up with him as he sprinted down the narrow passageway, then right through a door into a stairwell. We followed it up two flights to a matching door, which he peered out of again. It led onto a wide, carpeted corridor as we exited the servants' area. The corridor was empty, he ran diagonally across it to a large cream and gold door, grabbing the handle.

It was locked. He tried frantically, rattling the handle. He took three steps back then launched at the door with his foot at the lock. It made a tremendous noise but the door stayed firm.

He looked at me in panic.

'Together,' I told him.

We both took three steps back, nodded at each other and went for it with everything we had. There was a deafening crack as the lock broke through the wooden frame. I felt a smaller crack in my leg and collapsed in agony. Amal dragged me through the door by my shoulders and shut it behind us.

He rolled up my trousers and checked my lower leg.

'Probably just a fracture,' he tried to reassure me. 'Can you walk?'

'I can hop.'

I hobbled into the bedroom and rested on the bed whilst Amal disappeared into Rania's walk-in wardrobe. Resting my leg on the floor sent pain shooting up my body, holding it off the ground caused it to start shaking. I moved further onto the bed until both legs were stretched out in front of me.

From this angle I could see over my shoulder to the window, and through it beyond the walls to a street empty of traffic or civilians. In the middle of the road there was a checkpoint, the road running either side of its little shelter, with a barrier across each lane. Standing at a barrier was one policeman, and leaning in the shelter smoking a cigarette, one soldier. I watched as the soldier received a message on his radio and replied with one word. Then he carefully took the cigarette from his mouth and placed it on a ledge, exited the shelter towards the policeman, raised his rifle, and shot him twice in the chest. The policeman fell straight on his back. His hand was still twitching by his side when the soldier stood over him and fired one more shot into his face. Then he slung his rifle over his shoulder and dragged the policeman by the boot into the little shelter, out of sight below window level, where he returned the cigarette to his mouth.

I scrambled off the bed with agonising effort and over to the glass. There was still nothing, and no one else, on the road. I looked down at the ground between the palace and the walls. Nestled in the gap was an idling black Mercedes. I looked back over the walls to the road, a convoy of military transports had rounded the end of the street and was approaching the now army-manned checkpoint.

Amal returned with two Chandors (full-length cloaks to be held together at the front) and two Hijabs (head-scarves). We wrapped our heads as best we could, leaving only our eyes and noses visible, and threw the cloaks round our shoulders; they did not quite reach the floor and we had to stoop to hide our male shoes. I showed him the Mercedes and told him to follow me.

Once again he poked his head out into the corridor, it was still empty, so we moved back into the servants' stairwell and down to the ground floor, then back out into the small passageway, across into a small kitchen, and over to the window, outside of which the Mercedes was idling.

It took both of us to pull up the window. Munir's eyes bulged with happiness when he recognised us. We leant out of the window, he opened the car door and skipped the three metres between us. He waded into the bush below the window just to give me a hug.

'Sir, you're alive!' he cried. He did not seem to notice Amal.

'I can't believe you're here,' I told him.

'I wasn't going to leave you a second time. Quickly,

get in.'

'We can't, the army are almost here, they'll search any car that comes out.'

'The army? What's going on?'

'We're getting out by a tunnel that comes out at a guard house to the south of the walls. If you can get out, we need you to meet us there.'

'Get in the trunk, sir, I'll smuggle you out, it's safer.'

'I'm pretty sure they'll search the boot, Munir. We'll meet you at the guard house.'

I shut the window to avoid argument. Then Amal supported me as he walked and I hobbled across the room and back out into the corridor. We went up one floor and stayed in the empty servants' passages to get from the east wing to the west, but we had no choice not to enter back into the main corridors to approach the audience room. We stepped round the blood-strewn bodies of palace servants and government workers, fallen in the wide boulevards on their fronts and backs. The walls and doors were punctured and pockmarked.

I realised we were going to have to cross the red-carpeted landing at the top of the main stairs. Amal poked his scarf-wrapped head out. We were at a front corner, and would have to walk parallel to the stairs as they rose up to meet the floor, then across the top of them to the corner diagonally across from us. Right now, the landing was empty.

We moved out, shuffling with a stoop to keep the cloaks around us. As we moved parallel with the stairs the main entrance hall slowly revealed itself below us. A crowd of fifty people were seated on the carpet, all well-dressed palace and government employees, surrounding them were army men with rifles aimed over their heads, and surrounding them were the strewn bodies of slain invaders. I could spot Daniel's grey head in the middle of it all, he appeared to have a broken nose. All they had to do to spot us was look up.

We stopped by the top of the stairs. Making it across would be impossible without someone catching us in the corner of their eye.

Just as I was thinking that we might make it if we crawled on our bellies, there came the distant hum of a helicopter. The soldiers and the huddled group raised their heads to follow the noise, we ducked, then it became a roar as the Black Hawk appeared in the air outside the main entrance, over the parked cars, throwing sand through the open doors. A space had been cleared for it, and the moment its tyres hit the ground General Othman leapt down from it, flanked by guards with assault rifles.

We ran across the landing, fear numbing the agony from my leg. We disappeared into a corridor, leaping over the body of a woman whose lower back was soaked with blood. She grabbed at my cloak, but I snatched it from her grasp and kept moving.

We made it into the audience chamber, over to a small alcove covered by a curtain. When Amal pulled back the curtain it revealed a heavy wooden door, battered and chipped by ancient weapons, and with the lock freshly smashed. Amal hauled it open, pushed me in, pulled the curtain back, and closed the door.

It was utterly black inside. I could feel cold stone on my fingertips and the air was cool. I pulled Amal's phone from my pocket to light the passage, but it only showed us three metres of ghostly stone disappearing into darkness. We got moving.

'The British built this tunnel,' his voice echoed behind me, 'to smuggle officers out in the event of an uprising. My grandfather used it to smuggle prostitutes in.'

After two minutes of limping there was silky light bleeding from the end of the tunnel. As we got closer it formed into a grid, the tunnel opening into a small chamber, formerly sealed by a portcullis that had been raised just enough to crawl under. Amal ran to it, but I pulled him back just as the shadow of a soldier swept across.

He seemed to be alone. He paced one way across the portcullis, disappeared, then paced back the other way. The process was repeated. A rifle was slung over his shoulder, and a cigarette dangled limply from his lip.

Beyond him we could see a dirt street and dilapidated buildings. We could hear traffic. We were so close.

Amal put his hand on mine, he wanted us to go for it, do whatever we could. I nodded sombrely; we had no other choice. Just as we dug our feet into the ground, we heard the screech of brakes and the black Mercedes skidded to a stop just beyond the bars. The solider instantly aimed his rifle at it. Munir stepped out with his hands up, pleading desperately with the man in Arabic.

'He's saying his sisters are inside,' Amal whispered. He grabbed me by the arm and we shuffled into the light a few feet from the portcullis.

Munir begged the man some more. The solider was young, and confused. Then Munir ran to the boot and opened it. The soldier was jumpy, raising his rifle again. Munir returned with two big cartons of cigarettes, thrusting them onto the boy, who took them reluctantly and shouted at us to hurry.

Amal went first, scrabbling under the iron spikes. I followed as quickly as I could with my injured leg. It was impossible to keep our cloaks tightly round us, and I am sure the soldier saw that we were men, but after I had hobbled to my feet and climbed into the back of the car, instead of looking angry, he looked scared, as though he did not want the trouble.

I watched him through the tinted back window as

Munir sped us down the dirt street, weighing the cigarettes in his hands. Just as we turned the corner, he threw them on the ground and reached for his radio.

LAST CHAPTER

The Lone and Level Sands

'WE NEED TO SWITCH CARS,' I announced to both of them as we zipped through the streets, Amal and I pulling off our cloaks and head-scarves. 'A government car is too conspicuous. Munir, do you have your own car?'

'No, sir, sorry.'

'Do you know anywhere we can get one? We'll trade this one for any car that runs.'

'My brother, sir, is that ok?'

'Perfect.'

He turned us onto a main road where we soon hit traffic. Something was holding everyone up. As we moved three car lengths forwards, a truck did a U-turn five spaces in front, revealing a military checkpoint. Munir quickly copied the truck and we turned back down the other way. We then took a left into a small side street, we kept on this direction for several blocks until we hit the outskirts, only then did Munir turn the car back west.

After a mile of kicking sand at mud houses, we entered back into a stone and concrete district. We took a left, turning back in towards the city centre, but we were still outside it when we pulled to a stop at a half-concrete half-clay two storey house along a dirt alley just wide enough for the Mercedes.

'Wait here,' Munir instructed us as he got out, leaving the engine running, but locking the doors.

We could see a boxy orange hatchback parked in an open-ended garage that ran under the house. Munir banged on the front door. It swung open, unlocked. He stepped into the shadows inside, disappearing from our view.

The street was too quiet. I looked up through the tinted glass to the first floor window of the house opposite. Framed there, was a small girl. She reached out her tiny index finger to point at us and mouth something. She looked over her shoulder into the room. Then her mother appeared at the window. She stared at the car for some moments, then picked the girl up into her arms and reached out to close the latticed wooden window shutters.

Gusts of wind blew sand down the alley in waves. Little dunes formed at the bottom of the windscreen. The sand in the air obscured the long view ahead, the alley stretching for at least two hundred metres without any intersections. I looked out the back and down the dirt path to the T-junction where we entered. The only thing opposite was a bare stone wall. On it fluttered the ghostly projection of a flag's shadow, and the outline of the building in front. They were the only shadows. I stared at the flag as it continued to ripple in the breeze.

I ran the electric window down just an inch. On the hot wind came a gentle rumble. I craned my head onto its side to look up at the tiny shaft of sky I could see between the car ceiling and the front of the house next to us. Into that blue shaft came the dancing black dot of a helicopter.

'Where's Munir?' I asked.

'I can't see, he went inside.'

I looked out the back again. The flag was still alone. Then the shadow of a head and shoulders rose up just below it, just over the outline of the building in front. There was a sudden scratching at my window, I turned at it in terror, two dark yellow eyes looked in at me. It was a dog; scratching at the door, jumping, trying to sniff at the open window.

There was still no sign of Munir. I opened my door and stepped out. The dog jumped at me, then jumped into the car. At standing height I could see the flag on the nearby roof. It was a tattered, faded, colourless Argolisian flag, bleached by the sun. A boy sat on the roof